Wedded for His Royal Duty

—

Susan Meier

H HARLEQUIN® ROMANCE

Recycling programs
for this product may
not exist in your area.

ISBN-13: 978-0-373-74392-6

Wedded for His Royal Duty

First North American Publication 2016

Copyright © 2016 by Linda Susan Meier

Printed in U.S.A.

www.Harlequin.com

Susan Meier is the author of over fifty books for Harlequin. *The Tycoon's Secret Daughter* was a Romance Writers of America RITA® Award finalist, and *Nanny for the Millionaire's Twins* won the Book Buyers Best Award and was a finalist in the National Readers' Choice Awards. She is married and has three children. One of eleven children, she loves to write about the complexity of families and totally believes in the power of love.

Books by Susan Meier

Harlequin Romance

The Princes of Xaviera

Pregnant with A Royal Baby!

The Vineyards of Calanetti

A Bride for the Italian Boss

Mothers in a Million

A Father for Her Triplets

The Larkville Legacy

The Billionaire's Baby SOS

Kisses on Her Christmas List
The Tycoon's Secret Daughter
Nanny for the Millionaire's Twins
Single Dad's Christmas Miracle
Daring to Trust the Boss
The Twelve Dates of Christmas
Her Brooding Italian Boss

Visit the Author Profile page
at Harlequin.com for more titles.

To my readers... You inspire me to always write the best stories for you!

CHAPTER ONE

PRINCE ALEXANDROS SANCHO drove his horse up a thin path that wound through the woods behind the palace grounds of his family's estate. Thor moved with the speed and agility of a true champion, creating a tunnel of wind that swirled around them.

Normally, Alex would be on the beach right now. Enjoying the bikini-clad beauties showing off their toned and tan bodies, pretending they were oblivious to the attention they drew.

With his ever-present bodyguards dressed as tourists, standing strategically around him, and a steady stream of friends at the ready, he'd swim a bit, have lunch, gamble, take a nap and then shower to start all over again.

First, he'd hit the casinos to see if he could find a woman who suited his mood as a companion for the evening, then they'd have dinner, maybe gamble some more and let the night take them where it would.

He nudged Thor to go faster. Today, he couldn't do any of the things he loved to do. Least of all find a willing female. No. Today was the day he would officially meet the woman he would marry.

The *princess*.

He all but spat the word in his mind as the wind caressed him, trying to soothe him and failing. He'd seen pictures of her, of course. Through the years, they'd also unofficially run into each other at boarding school. But she was several years younger, and he'd met her believing she'd be marrying his older brother Dominic as part of a treaty. So their greetings had been stilted, though polite. After boarding school, their paths never crossed again. She'd attended university in the United States where she'd taken up causes—everything from starving children to stray cats.

He struggled not to squeeze his eyes shut in frustration. Dominic had gotten a one-night stand pregnant, and he'd married Ginny because their son was the next heir to Xaviera's throne, which made Alex the only prince available to fulfill the terms of the treaty with Grennady. Princess Eva had turned twenty-five a few months before. She was officially marriage age, and his time of doing what he wanted, when he wanted, was up.

Even worse, she would be Grennady's queen one day. Marrying a crusader who would be queen seemed apt punishment for a prince who'd spent his life avoiding responsibility.

With another nudge to Thor, he sent the horse galloping toward the stable, only slowing the pace when they got close to the wide wooden barn door. He jumped off and tossed his riding crop to a servant girl milling about the building. Her faded blue jeans and T-shirt showed off a fantastic figure, but it was her dark hair and pale blue-gray eyes that made his hormones sit up and take notice.

Any other day, he'd flirt, itching to run his hands through the shiny black locks that probably reached her bottom when they weren't hiked up in a ponytail. But, today, he was about to meet his future bride.

"Thor gets the star treatment," he said, taking off the black helmet that matched his black leather boots and gloves. "Don't think you can scrimp with brushing. I'll be back this evening after tonight's dinner party to make sure he's been properly cared for."

The woman looked at him in bewilderment.

He sighed. "I know. He's an Arabian with four white boots. Bad luck if you want to breed him."

"But I'm—"

"New. I get it." And he didn't want to stand around chatting. Especially not with a beautiful woman, who only reminded him of everything he was tossing away because of his family's misplaced sense of duty. "Off with you, now. I have business."

Princess Eva Latvaia looked at the riding crop in her hands, then Prince Alex Sancho's back as he walked away from her. Sweat caused his white-and-tan polo shirt to stick to his skin, displaying unexpectedly toned muscles. He ran his fingers through his gorgeous, thick curly black hair.

At least their children would be getting good genes.

She shook her head and took Thor's reins. "A fine name for you, sir. A child of the gods."

The great horse whinnied.

Eva laughed. She said, "You're a misfit," but she stroked his nose to take the sting out of it. "So am I."

Thor shook his head.

"How'd you end up in a palace?"

One of the stable employees raced out of the open double doors. He grabbed the reins in Eva's hands. "I'm so sorry, Princess." He bowed.

She straightened regally, aware of her position, but she also smiled. "This is what I get for taking a stroll when I should be getting ready for a party."

The older gentleman chuckled and turned to walk Thor into the stable.

Eva had heard the Sancho household was different. She supposed having a new baby around was part of it. But she'd also heard that the woman who'd married Dominic, the prince Eva had been dreaming of since she was four, had brought a more relaxed attitude to the royal family.

And now Eva had to face Dom tonight—and his princess—the woman who'd basically stolen him from Eva. In a way, his marrying someone else was good. She was next in line for her throne. So was he. Theirs would have been a difficult life and a difficult marriage. Still, she'd been dreaming of Dom since she was old enough to watch *Cinderella*, in love with the idea of marrying a handsome prince and ruling their countries together. Her whole world had worked itself out in her head. And now—

Now, add losing Dom to what her father had done, and everything was off. Wrong. Almost unbearable.

Head high, she walked back to the palace. She rode the elevator to the fourth floor and the guest apartment she'd been given for her stay. She opened just one door of the elegant double-door entrance, and strode through the high-ceilinged foyer to the sitting room, where her mother picked a chocolate from the tray provided as a welcome gift from the king. It seemed she'd replaced crying with eating.

"You're not going to fit into your mother-of-the-bride dress for the wedding if you keep eating those."

Her mom, a short thin woman with hair as black as Eva's, offered the candy to her. "They're divine. You should try them."

"Then both of us will need a bigger size dress."

Eva's mother dropped the chocolate back to the tray. "You're right. I want to look nice. I want your derelict of a father to feel bad for leaving me. And I want to prove at least some of us take our royal duties to heart."

Eva sat on the sofa. "I'm glad to see you're feeling better, Mom."

"Running away with an aide." She shook her head. "Seriously. Could he be any more cliché?"

"It's not exactly cliché to give up your throne." He hadn't officially put down his crown, but a royal divorce came with consequences. Running away with another woman meant a divorce would soon follow, and her dad would no longer be king. Then she would be queen. At twenty-five years old, she'd have the weight of a country on her shoulders. She couldn't believe her father had done this to her—and for a mistress.

She thanked God that the Sancho family had insisted they fulfill the terms of the treaty that promised her in marriage to one of King Ronaldo's sons. At least she had this way of bringing herself into the good graces of their subjects before she took the crown. Even if she wasn't getting the prized prince, the son who would be king, she would prove she would do her duty to her country even when things were crumbling around her, by upholding the terms of a treaty that ensured oil and safe passage for Grennady's tankers.

"I wonder if he's coming to the wedding."

"Your dad?" Her mom winced. "Great. Thanks for reminding me that he might. Now I really do have to give up chocolates." She tossed the candy tray to the coffee table. "While you were out, did you hear any palace gossip about when the wedding will occur?"

"Xaviera's servants are a happy, obviously well-cared-for staff, and they are incredibly closemouthed."

Her mom rose from the sofa. "I guess we'll find out tonight."

"I guess we will."

As her mother turned and walked to her bedroom, Eva headed in the opposite direction to the second bedroom.

Having lived in America for seven years, she no longer had a maid draw her bath. She relished the simple pleasure of running water, adding scented oils and luxuriating—alone— for twenty minutes.

But remembering the way Alexandros had thought her a servant girl, she called for the palace hairdresser. She had housekeeping steam her gown to make sure there wasn't a hint of a wrinkle.

That evening, when she stepped out of her room and into the apartment's sitting area, her mom gasped. "Oh, Eva! Are you sure red is a good idea? And strapless? Showing your shoulders when you meet a king and your future husband? They could think you a tart."

With a quick nod of approval for her mom's sedate blue gown that showed off her thin figure and suited her black hair, she said, "Alexandros already mistook me for a servant girl."

"What?"

"I ran into Alex when I took a walk to the stables. He handed me his riding crop, told me to take care of his horse."

Her mom gaped in horror.

"I want to see the look on his face when he realizes who I am."

"Is it that or are you trying to make Prince Dominic jealous?"

Eva stopped halfway to the sofa, her heart rattling around in her chest. She'd loved Prince Dominic from the day she'd found his picture in the newspaper and her mom had told her he was the boy she would be marrying. While other girls crushed on rock stars and soccer players, she'd happily shown everyone the picture of her handsome prince. She never had to feel bad if she didn't get invited to a dance or if boys ignored her at a party. She had her prince.

And he'd married someone else.

She swallowed hard, as humiliation bubbled through her, but when she faced her mother she wore a happy smile. Her mom had enough misery of her own. She didn't need to be further upset over how uncomfortable this situation was for Eva.

"Now, wouldn't I be silly to be pining over a man I didn't even know?"

Her mother eyed her shrewdly. "You're sure?"

"I'm positive."

She seemed to buy that, but Eva's breath gave a funny catch. What was it going to feel like not just meeting Dominic, but meeting the woman who had stolen him right out from under her?

A member of the palace guard arrived and escorted them to the king's private quarters. The king himself and his new wife, Queen Rose, greeted them.

King Ronaldo took Eva's hand and kissed it. "It is such a pleasure to meet you as an adult, Princess."

Eva smiled graciously and curtsied. "The honor is mine, Your Majesty."

"This is my new wife, Rose. She's Princess Ginny's mom. She and Dominic aren't here yet, but you know how new babies are. They don't always adhere to schedules." He laughed. "Anyway, Queen Rose, may I present Princess Eva Latavia of Grennady."

Eva curtsied again. "A pleasure to meet you."

Queen Rose, a tall blonde with just a hint of pink in her hair and a very obvious Texas twang, waved her hand in dismissal. "Oh, none of that for me." She suddenly enveloped Eva in a hug. "This is the way we welcome people into the family in Texas." She pulled back and looked Eva in the eye. "You're familiar, right? You were educated in the US?"

"Yes, ma'am," Eva said, mimicking the Southern drawl she'd heard the entire time she was at Florida State.

Rose laughed. "That's my girl!"

King Ronaldo turned to Eva's mother. "And this is your mom? Queen Karen, correct?"

Eva's heart swelled with gratitude when the king mentioned nothing of her father's potential abdication of the throne and still gave her mom the respect of the title Queen.

Her mother curtsied. "Your Majesty."

He bowed. "It's my honor to meet you." He motioned to Rose. "And this is Queen Rose."

Karen curtsied again. "A pleasure to meet you."

Rose chuckled. "I know you people like your

official greetings, but I'm just a hugger." She gave Karen a big squeeze.

The king directed everyone into a drawing room with a bar.

Eva looked around in unabashed curiosity. She knew some royals were wealthier than others. Xaviera's location alone gave them access to oil money. But this palace was amazing. The art so casually displayed on the walls was probably worth the gross national product of Grennady.

Her mom leaned in and whispered to her daughter, "So, the mom of the last princess ended up married to the king. Maybe this won't be such a bad deal after all?"

Eva couldn't stop a giggle that escaped. "Behave."

"Rose doesn't."

"She's the queen. That gives her license to be eccentric."

"Right."

The king motioned to the bar. "Can I get anyone anything?"

Karen said, "I'd love a wine spritzer."

"Princess Eva?"

"I'd like—"

But before she could name her wine choice, Alexandros rose from behind the bar. Dressed in the royal uniform of their country, black trousers with a red jacket filled with medals, he looked totally different than the guy in the riding breeches, white-and-tan shirt and scuffed helmet.

His dark eyes met hers, and the bottle of wine he held fell to the bar top.

She smiled.

King Ronaldo said, "I understand you've met Alex in school."

Holding the gaze of his dark eyes, she said, "And we met this afternoon. Accidentally. At the stables."

Rose said, "Oh! You ride." She winced. "Of course you do. It was probably part of your training. I'd love to go out with you one of these mornings."

Polite and proper, Eva faced Rose. "I'd like that too."

King Ronaldo said, "Funny. Alex didn't mention seeing you this afternoon."

Feeling her pride return, Eva spared Alex a glance before returning her gaze to the king. "I don't think he knew who I was."

Alex felt his face redden like a teenager's.

"He handed me his riding crop and told me to make sure his horse got the star treatment."

The king gasped. "Alexi!"

"Well, she didn't look like this," Alex said, pointing at her red gown and dark hair pinned up just enough to get it off her face while the rest spilled over her shoulders and fell in thick curls down her bare back. He thought of all that black hair fanned out on a white pillow and almost dropped the wine again.

Eva casually said, "Perhaps he was just pre-occupied."

The king said, "Perhaps," but Alex stared at her red dress. The strapless top hugged her breasts and cruised to her tiny waist, before it flared out in a skirt made up of yards and yards of some kind of filmy material. It didn't bell out. It just flowed smoothly, effortlessly with every one of her graceful movements.

He didn't know what he'd expected from this woman he'd met when she was little more than a child, but it wasn't this grace. Or this sensuality. It was as if she was telling the world that she might someday be a queen, but she was also a sexy woman.

Her lips lifted into a knowing smile.

She had him stumbling all over himself, and she liked it.

No. She reveled in it. And he supposed he couldn't blame her. His family had yanked the good prince away from her and forced her to take him or nothing. Only a week after her own father had disgraced their crown, the Sancho family had decided it was time to make good on the terms of their treaty, forcing her to marry a lesser prince, then he hadn't recognized her at the stable that afternoon. She wasn't insulting him by telling everybody he'd thought her a stable girl. She was repairing her royal pride.

The door of the drawing room opened and Alex's gaze shifted as his brother and his wife arrived, and for the second time that evening he was struck speechless. Princess Ginny walked in on Dominic's arm, wearing the same gown as Eva, except Ginny's was a soft, romantic gray.

Dominic said, "Sorry we're late."

King Ronaldo and Queen Rose immediately shifted in their direction.

Rose said, "Is something wrong with Jimmy? Is he sick?"

Ginny laughed. "No, Mom. Your grandson is fine."

Princess Eva stood in front of the bar, motionless, as if stunned into silence, watching the happy couple.

Alex leaned forward, across the gleaming

wooden surface. "Well, now. What have we here? You and Ginny in the same gown. Except yours is red and hers is a pretty gray. Very innocent and sweet. While yours is…well, on the trashy side. It's kind of like looking at those devil and angel pictures."

He saw her back stiffen and knew he'd struck a nerve. Good. She hadn't even tried to tell him who she was at the stable that afternoon. She'd taken his crop. Led him to believe she'd be caring for Thor. Let him walk away. And then embarrassed him in front of his father.

"Shut up."

He watched the muscles of her bare back shift as she straightened, composing herself. But he still saw the tension and knew his golden opportunity for getting even wasn't over yet.

"Oh, don't get me wrong. I don't mind one bit being the brother to marry the devilish princess. I'm just not exactly sure this was the first impression you wanted to make on the guy who dumped you."

"He didn't dump me."

"He isn't exactly marrying you."

"He's already married."

"And to somebody who looks like your polar opposite. Isn't that interesting?"

He saw vulnerability flicker in her gray-blue eyes as Dominic and Ginny approached her. He didn't really know Eva, but he did know what it was like to be second best. To be the one not chosen. To be the one who stood behind his brother and dad, a king and a man who would be king.

His chest clenched. She might be educated. She might be a tough crusader who could speak up for those who didn't have a voice, but nothing could have prepared her for meeting the woman who'd stolen her fiancé from her.

She was too damned pretty to be Dominic's second. Alex wasn't anybody's knight in shining armor, but he did know a thing or two about fooling people into believing he was fine. Happy. That his life was perfect. And that was what Eva needed right now. To be rescued from an embarrassing situation that befuddled her so much that even the royal pride she'd just gathered was sinking fast.

He raced around the bar. Sliding his arm along her waist, he whispered, "Here's the story…when we met at the stables this afternoon there was an instant attraction."

She met his gaze. "Really?"

"Would you rather be somebody who unexpectedly found herself crazy about me, or the woman left behind by my big brother?"

Her head tilted in confusion.

"Don't be the one left behind in the dust. Leave *him* behind."

"*Oh.*"

"You don't have a lot of experience with men, do you?"

"I've been engaged since I was four."

"And I guess now you're going to tell me you're a virgin."

She said nothing, just held his gaze.

"Well, I'll be damned."

"You'll absolutely be damned," Dom said as he reached them. He held out his hand and Princess Eva presented her hand to him. He kissed the knuckles. "Princess Eva. It's nice to see you. I'm so sorry we're meeting again under awkward circumstance."

Like a champ, she slid her arm beneath Alex's and stepped closer to him. "There's no reason to be concerned. We've barely spoken to each other. Besides, I was lucky enough to meet Alex this afternoon at the stables."

Alex winked at her. "Love at first sight."

Dom said, "Really?"

Alex laughed. "All right. Maybe lust at first sight."

Eva shifted her attention to Ginny. "And you must be the woman who stole Dom's heart." She smiled. "You have lovely taste in clothes."

Alex had trouble stifling a laugh. Still, from the way she'd put him in his place for not recognizing her, he should have expected she could hold her own. She'd simply needed help getting over the awkwardness of seeing Dom.

Ginny laughed and glanced down at her gown. "You have good taste too. Maybe better. That red is divine."

"Alex told me I looked like a devil in this dress."

"And that you looked like an angel," Alex said to Ginny. He kissed Eva's cheek. "But you know I'd always rather have the devil."

"So," Dom said, looking from Alex to Eva, appearing not quite convinced. "Things worked out for the best?"

Alex tightened his arm around her waist. "We think so."

A servant quietly shuffled into the room and whispered something in King Ronaldo's ear. He nodded once. When the servant was gone, the king faced the two couples at the bar.

"Dinner is served. If you'll all follow me to the dining room."

Dom and Ginny immediately got in line behind his father, but Eva caught Alex's arm to hold him back. When the room was empty she said, "I owe you."

He couldn't help it. He grinned. She might be able to hold her own, but she'd needed him to get over that awkward introduction. "Yes, you do. I just saved you months of embarrassment—maybe years if the press decided to make an issue of Dom marrying someone else—and I have the perfect way for you to pay me back."

CHAPTER TWO

EVA'S HEART CHUGGED in her chest. After Alex's good guess about her virginity, she couldn't imagine what he had in mind as payback, but she did know she owed him. So when he asked her to meet him at the stables at midnight, she hadn't argued. She'd simply enjoyed the dinner, keeping up Alex's pretense that their chance meeting that afternoon had sparked an instant attraction. Then she'd said polite goodbyes to the king and his new wife and Dom and his wife, before she walked her mom back to their quarters, changed into jeans and a lightweight sweater and headed for the stable.

The moon rose high in the sky. A faint ocean breeze lured her down the cobblestone path. An island in the Mediterranean, Xaviera had January temps that were much warmer than the climate of her country, which was nestled between Finland and Russia. If she were home right now, she'd be wearing boots and a parka and battling a winter wind to get to her stables.

She reached the big stone-and-wood building and entered through a door on the side. Though the stable was the cleanest she'd ever seen, the earthy scents of horse, hay and leather hit her. She glanced down the long row of stalls and saw Alex standing in front of the last one, petting the nose of his Arabian, Thor.

She strode down the aisle.

Alex heard her and smiled. "So you've come to dicker."

"I didn't come to negotiate anything. I came to see what my payback will be for you saving me tonight."

He laughed. "It's odd to hear somebody say that. Usually I'm the one who has to make amends."

"Quite a reputation my future husband has."

"Actually, that's the point. The best way you can pay me back is to not marry me."

She gasped. "I have to marry you!"

He bobbed his head, as if thinking through her comment, then said, "Not really."

"We have a treaty!"

"Made decades ago." He caught her gaze. "Were you mature enough at age four to commit to someone?"

He knew the answer to that so she said nothing.

"Of course, you weren't. And then we pulled the rug out from under you. The prince you were supposed to marry is now married to someone else. You're not getting the prince who was promised to you. You're not even getting the good prince, the one who will someday be king. You're getting second-best."

She looked at him, wearing a T-shirt with the front tucked into nice-fitting jeans, with his dark curly hair casually messed, and those intriguing brown eyes. For a beat of time, she wondered if she really was getting second-best. Dominic was handsome in the perfect, strait-laced way. This guy? Alex? He was rough-around-the-edges gorgeous. A sexy bad boy. And all hers in a few months—

She swallowed hard as strange tingling sensations cruised through her.

She ignored them. When all was said and done, this was about duty. Oil and safe passage for their tankers trumped which prince she would actually marry. And needing to make herself look strong and loyal to her country trumped both of those.

"I don't have a choice."

He walked toward her. "Actually, I read the

agreement and the treaty. *You* might not have a choice. *I* might not have a choice. But *we* have a choice. If both of us decide not to marry, we can nullify it."

She gaped at him. "Nullify a treaty? Just because you don't want to marry me?"

"I don't want to get married at all. And we wouldn't be nullifying the whole treaty, just that one clause." He sighed. "Look, I rescued you tonight because it's not right that somebody as pretty as you are should be perceived as an also-ran, the woman who didn't make the cut."

Her pulse slowed, then speeded up again. Forget all about Dominic dumping her. Forget about the treaty. Alex thought she was pretty? He was one of the most eligible bachelors in the world and she was a woman whose dad had tossed their family into an unfathomable scandal. Alex should be running from her as fast as his feet would take him. Instead, he thought she was pretty? Too pretty to be known as the princess who didn't make the cut.

"But I'm not anybody's knight in shining armor."

He hadn't mentioned her father's betrayal, or the fact that she'd soon become a queen, but she was well aware of both and the consequences. Alex might not want to rescue her, but he was her only option to show her subjects that her family still remembered their call to service.

She lifted her chin. "Like it or not, you have to be mine. Or your country is in violation of our treaty."

"I told you we can—"

"No! My father disgraced us enough! I have to prove I will do my duties!"

His eyes narrowed. His full lips pursed. "You're refusing my plan."

"Yes."

He stepped closer. Instinct told her to step back. Common sense told her he'd see that as a sign of weakness. So she held her ground, looked him in the eyes, as he circled her, inspecting her as if she were his next purchase. Waves and waves of chill bumps trickled down her spine.

"Why would a girl as pretty as you are want to marry someone she doesn't really know?"

"I told you I have to—"

"Prove you'll do your duty," he interrupted her. "Got it. And I believe that's part of it." He stopped at her side and slid his hand under the thick lock of hair that fell over her shoulder to her breast. Running the silken strands through his fingers, he said, "I would think you'd be eager to find somebody your own age. Maybe somebody who shared your interest in land mines and whatnot."

"First, I'm not part of the land mine fight. Second, you are my age. Five years isn't that much of a difference."

He flipped the strand of hair over her shoulder, and the tingles that rained down on her when his fingers brushed her skin nearly made her shiver.

"So you like me?"

"I didn't say that."

He smiled knowingly, stepped close. "Just attracted then."

"To you?" She'd meant for it to sound like a scoff. It came out as a squeak.

"Or maybe you're simply not clear about what attraction is. Being a virgin and all."

If the feelings tumbling around her right now were attraction, then he was correct. This crazy combination of fear that he'd touch her again and longing to feel his fingers graze her skin totally confused her. Her chest was tight. Her body wanted to shiver. Even her lips tingled.

"I've had boyfriends."

"So you wouldn't mind if I kissed you."

"As a way to get me to drop the idea of marrying you? How badly do you kiss?"

She'd barely gotten the word *kiss* out of her mouth before he grabbed her by the shoulders, drew her to him and planted his lips on hers. The shock of it buckled her knees. His arm fell to her waist, anchoring her against him as wave after wave of warmth flowed through her. But as quickly as he'd yanked her to him, he released her.

She stared at him. Her nerve endings glowed like the sparks from a Roman candle. She couldn't quite get air into her lungs.

He grinned.

Not sure what to say, what to do, she fell back on dignity. As haughtily as possible, she said, "I'm still marrying you," before she turned on her heel and walked out of the stable.

Head high, she marched up the cobblestone path so afraid he was following her that her neck hurt from fighting the urge to look behind her.

When she reached her quarters, she breathed a sigh of relief, though her hands shook and her knees still wobbled.

Her mother awaited her on the sofa. "So how did it go?"

How did it go? In twenty seconds, he'd reduced her limbs to jelly, and no matter how hard she tried she couldn't get her heart to stop thumping.

"He doesn't want to marry me. He says if we both say we want to step away from the marriage, that section of the treaty will be nullified."

Her mother gasped. "Oh, no! Our family has disgraced our country enough! You have to do something to prove you're still loyal enough to the crown to do your duty!"

She fell to the sofa beside her mom. "I know. I told him that."

But convincing him of her duty was only part of her problem. One twenty-second kiss had thrown her for a loop. Made her feel hot and cold. Changed her breathing. Given her chill bumps. When she'd pictured marrying Dominic, the images were warm and sweet. When she thought of marrying Alex, the images became hot and steamy.

And, oh, dear God, she was *not* a hot and steamy girl.

"Our family has been respected as leaders of Grennady for centuries. But your father has put us in a precarious position. You cannot look weak or wishy-washy. You cannot walk away from a treaty mere weeks before you become queen. The press will crucify you. Your entire reign will be tainted."

Eva's brain tried to pay attention to her mom but couldn't. She couldn't stop thinking about how experienced Alex was and how little she knew. How did a virgin please a playboy?

Her mother grabbed her hands. "You've got to marry Alex."

Her chest filled with anxiety. There was no good option here. If she returned to her country without marrying Alex, it would appear she had no respect for treaties. If she married Alex, she was so far out of her depth she'd most likely make both of them miserable.

"I don't think he's going to give up on trying to get me to bow out."

"Then you have to make him like you."

Right. Leave it to her mom to reduce this to something that sounded simple but really wasn't.

She took a breath. "How exactly do I do that?"

"Flirt. Compliment him. Women have been doing it for centuries."

Every woman but Eva. In high school, she'd only dated boys who were friends. As an adult, she gone out with men who knew she was promised to a prince and would have thought it odd if she flirted. Worse, Alex had probably been flirted with by the best. If she got it wrong, or was clumsy, she'd make a fool of herself.

Still, she didn't have options. She *had to* go through with this marriage. Plus, it would be months before the actual wedding. There was time to fix this. Time for him to get to know her. Time for her to learn to flirt.

She just had to stop being smart with him and treat him with respect—

And Google flirting.

The next morning at six, Alex's phone rang. He groaned and rolled over, but when it rang again he recognized the ringtone as his father's. He sat up, ran his hand down his face and snatched his cell from the bedside table.

"Yes, Father."

"It's me, sweet pea," his stepmother Rose said cheerfully. "Your dad just realized that we never actually talked about the date for the wedding last night, and I thought it would be a good idea for all of us to have breakfast while we chat. So we can keep it light and friendly."

"Great."

"Great as in you will be there?" Without giving him a chance to reply, she said, "Thanks. You're a love."

She hung up the phone and Alex groaned again. The last thing he wanted to do was set a wedding date when he didn't want to get married. But marrying a woman who would be a queen? Somebody who'd keep him in the papers for real reasons, not just his winning streaks at the casinos or his escapades with women? Oh, man. That sucked.

Marrying somebody he didn't know because of a treaty was antiquated. Stupid. And he wouldn't do it. It was crazy to even consider marrying Eva. No matter how pretty she was.

He rose from the bed trying not to think about how her cheeks turned pink when he teased her or how hot that one quick kiss had been.

Because it had been hot. Ridiculously hot. Kissing someone who clearly hadn't been expecting to be kissed had been exciting. Challenging—

Hot. The hottest kiss he'd had in forever.

How long had it been since he'd had to woo a woman—

Damn it! He was thinking about her again. And he wasn't supposed to be thinking about her. He was supposed to be hatching a plan to get her to ditch this wedding.

He headed for the shower determined to get Eva out of his head, but what replaced her almost stopped his heart. The shadowy memory of his mom's death. His father falling apart. An entire palace full of servants weeping silently as they went about their duties.

He sucked in a breath, banishing the images, but in their place came other, more difficult visions. Memories of being told that his girlfriend, the first woman he'd really loved, had been killed in a boating accident. Vivid recollections of the soul-crushing grief that consumed him for nearly two years.

The loss had been so difficult that as the memories hit, he rubbed his chest to salve the ache always came when he thought of Nina.

Five years had passed, and he had gotten beyond Nina's death, so he told the images to go away. If his subconscious was reminding him of his mom and his first love because it was worried he could get feelings for Eva, it needn't have bothered. There was no way in hell he'd fall for a woman just because a treaty said he should. His subconscious could rest easy.

But he knew a royal summons when he got one. He couldn't refuse his father about this marriage. As a prince who'd very publicly enjoyed his royal lifestyle, he did not have the option of refusing. *Eva* had to refuse. Then he could tell his dad she was a virgin, and say he didn't want to force an innocent young woman to marry him. He'd look like the good guy. And his dad would agree.

That was the plan that would work, and that was the plan he was sticking to.

He dressed in lightweight slacks, a pale blue dress shirt—no tie—and navy sport coat, and headed for his father's elaborate quarters. He entered through the gold-trimmed doors into a foyer with high ceilings and Monet on the wall, and walked to the smaller dining room, the one his father used for informal breakfasts and lunches.

Rose immediately stood, raced to him and hugged him. After being without a mom since he was a boy, having her around was equal parts sweet and disruptive. Up until Ginny had gotten pregnant, this palace had been the home of men. Gold-trimmed and filled with precious art, but still a home of men. No women. No talk of babies or fashions—

"You look very dashing."

And no one commenting on his clothes unless he was inappropriately attired.

Luckily, he liked Rose. He was just grouchy because of this whole marriage mess. "Thanks."

"You and Eva will be seated there," his father said, pointing to the two chairs to his right. "We'll put your fiancée's mom on my left and Rose, of course, will sit across from me."

"No Dom and Ginny?"

"No need for Dom and Ginny to be here," his father said in his most kingly voice. "You're the one getting married."

He felt the noose tightening around his neck.

Escorted by his father's butler, Eva and her mom entered. Alex's mouth fell open. If he'd thought Eva a knockout in the red dress, the little white dress she wore tied his tongue. Simple and sweet, with some sort of short pink sweater thing, the dress shouldn't have made her look sexy. But there was something about the way the pink made her dark hair look even darker—or maybe the way the color set off her pale gray-blue eyes—

Damn it! What the hell was wrong with him? If he was noticing colors, it was definitely time to get out of this thing.

The butler bowed, announced Karen and Eva, and left the room.

Alex automatically pulled out the chair beside his for Eva. His father directed Karen to sit to his left.

As the king's attention was on offering the seat to his guest, Eva whispered, "Well, don't you look like the proper man about town?"

"Would you rather I came to breakfast in my robe and slippers?"

She laughed.

He frowned. "Where's the smart remark?"

She fiddled with her napkin. "No smart remarks today."

"Oh, come on. We both have reason to be unhappy about this wedding. Don't start playing Good Princess now."

"I am the good princess."

He didn't want to bring up her dad. Having a father abdicate his throne wasn't just embarrassing for a royal. It was humiliating. Still, he could use it without out-and-out saying it.

"You're about to become a queen. That's two huge life changes in the span of a couple of months. Too much for one person. Think this through."

"I don't have to think it through. Queens don't ignore treaties."

"Yeah, well, I don't want to get married."

She said nothing.

"And I'm going to do everything in my power to get you to agree."

She faced him, her eyes narrowed, as if accepting his challenge. "Great. Give it your best shot. Because I intend to convince you to marry me."

Alexi's tongue tied again. Her anger brightened her blue-gray eyes until they were almost silver, and sent a shiver down his spine. He skimmed his gaze over her hair, the pink tint in her cheeks, her lush mouth, and realized there absolutely were worse fates than being assigned to marry this woman.

Except she was a virgin, who was about to become a queen, and he didn't want to get married. He'd seen what happened to his father when his mom died. The king had crumbled from grief. And then there was his own loss. His first love—

Pain squeezed his heart. A wave of sorrow enveloped him.

That was why he'd thought of them this morning. Not to warn him that he could get feelings for Eva, but to remind him of why he didn't want to get close to *anyone*. The pain of loss was just too great to risk.

His father picked up his juice glass. "We

should have toasted this wedding last night, but we got a little preoccupied with baby talk."

Rose and Karen laughed.

The king raised his glass. "To the wedding that unites our two countries."

Everyone lifted his or her juice glass. "To the wedding that unites our two countries."

Alex said the words and drank his juice, but Eva could see his heart wasn't in it. A flame of anger licked at her soul. She was the virgin facing sleeping with a man she didn't know, a man experienced enough to have a harem, and *he* was unhappy?

She did not give a damn. She was going through with this wedding. Just as her mother said, she had to get him to like her.

He reached for a tray of fruit, and presented it to her. "Melon?"

"Yes."

Their eyes met, and thoughts of the kiss from the night before flooded her. The solidness of his body against hers when he yanked her to him, the press of his lips.

Though her breath hitched, she held his gaze. Intuition told her this was the time she should begin flirting, but not one cute or flirty thing came to mind. Her chest was so tight it was a wonder she could draw in air. She barely managed to say, "Thank you."

She scooped up a serving of the honeydew. When she handed the spoon to him, their fingers brushed and the memory of how he'd brushed her shoulder when he'd flipped her hair out of the way sent a shower of tingles down her spine.

He smiled. "Happy to see you're more nervous about our wedding today than you were yesterday."

"I'm not nervous about our wedding."

"Then what made your hand shake?"

There was absolutely no way in hell she'd tell him that remembering their ten minutes together the night before filled her with warmth. So she said nothing.

He looked away to serve himself some fruit. The sounds of good silver and elegant china filled the air. With the exception of her mom and Queen Rose discussing gardening, the room was quiet.

Alex said, "So how are your stray cats doing without you?"

Her chest loosened. Finally, something they could talk about. "They're fine." She risked a glance at him. "Thank you for asking."

"Don't they miss you when you're gone?"

"I started a few shelters that care for them. I don't need to be there twenty-four-seven... or even once a month. Every shelter is fully staffed, mostly with volunteers."

"That makes sense. Always good to have a staff in place."

"Yes. Especially when they are a competent staff. A staff that shares my vision." Eva relaxed a bit more. "I—" She caught the gaze of his dark eyes and almost lost her train of thought. It was no wonder he had the reputation with women that he had. He was gorgeous. His dark eyes had a lost, soulful quality that touched her heart in the weirdest way. And if they went through with this wedding, he would be hers. She would be married to one of the most gorgeous, richest men in the world. He could have his pick of women, but *she'd* be in his bed.

She sucked in a breath to banish those thoughts. If she let her brain leap ahead to their wedding night, she'd hyperventilate.

"I intend to start this kind of shelter in as many cities as I can."

"In the United States?"

She had his full attention. He was curious. And she was floundering because being near him was overwhelming. While he was cool and confident, she almost shook with emotions she didn't understand.

What she wouldn't give for the ability to flirt.

Maybe if she batted her eyelashes? Or smiled? *That was it. Maybe she should just smile? Instead of a big flirty move, she should just break the ice with a smile.*

She raised her lips, let the corners tip upward. "Yes. The problem doesn't seem to be as bad in my own country."

He tilted his head and studied her. "Interesting."

She hoped he was still talking about the cats. Because if he was making fun of her smiling at him, she would die. On the spot die. But not before she killed her mother for telling her to flirt with him.

"Being a rural country, Grennady has more barns and stables, places cats and dogs can find shelter in the winter."

"I see—" He held her gaze. The look in his eyes was so confusingly intense that she couldn't take another second. She let her gaze fall but when it did, it landed on his mouth—the mouth that had kissed her and changed her whole perspective about this arranged marriage.

Okay. Now she really was nervous. And felt hot and cold.

She yanked her gaze away from him and tried to focus on the main conversation at the table. King Ronaldo was discussing the latest thriller novel he was reading. She hoped to insert herself into that discussion, but no such luck. As her mother and Alex's father and stepmother found common ground in a book they'd all read, she and Alex were left behind like outsiders.

"So who's funding your shelter?"

"I am. I—"

She stopped. Her dad had been gone a little over a week. Her mother had only stopped crying the day before. She had gotten her monthly stipend the week before her dad left, but until her dad returned or made a decision there was no one to authorize the checks.

Good God. She might not be broke, but without her dad to approve her stipend, she had access to nothing.

She drew in a long, life-sustaining breath. She might not be penniless, but she might as well be.

"I *was* funding my shelter. With my allowance." She swallowed hard. "But, with my dad gone, there's no one to authorize my stipend."

She caught his gaze. "At least four shelters will have to close."

"That must have been some allowance."

Damn him for being such a twit! Her life was a mess and he was making jokes! "Thank you for making fun of me."

"I'm teasing you to lessen the awkwardness for you. I'm sorry about your dad."

She straightened her shoulders, sat up taller in her chair. She'd rather have him be a twit than feel sorry for her. "Nothing's official yet. He could take months before he actually divorces my mom…" And she'd be penniless until then.

The dining room doors opened again and a short, dark-haired woman entered. Dressed in a green business suit and simple taupe pumps, she carried a huge black book and a smaller one that could have been a calendar.

The king tapped his water glass to get everyone's attention. "Princess Eva, Queen Karen," he said, "This is Sally Peterson, our minister of protocol. She's here to officially set the date for the wedding."

Alex leaned in and whispered, "This date means nothing to me. All I'm finding out right now is how much time I have to try to convince you not to marry me."

Eva fumed. Her entire life had been turned upside down and he couldn't for two seconds pretend to do his royal duty. No. He had to keep rubbing it in that he wanted her gone.

Sally bowed and faced Eva. "Actually, Princess, your country gave us three dates. The second weekend in April."

Alex choked. Eva blanched. Even for someone willing to go through with this marriage, that wasn't very much time, not quite three months away. She had to convince Alex to marry her and get accustomed to the fact that she was getting married in three short months?

"The first week in March."

Alex picked up his water glass. Eva gaped at Sally Peterson. That was worse! Why were the dates so soon? So close?

"Or the second week in February, to coincide with Valentine's Day."

Four flipping weeks?

Eva coughed to cover her gasp of disbelief.

King Ronaldo said, "I like the February date. So that's our date." He rose from his seat. "Sally, perhaps you and the ladies would like to use this morning to talk about dresses and designers."

Rose rubbed her hands together with glee. "I'd love to! What do you say we take a pot of coffee into the living room and look at swatches and Google designers?"

Karen grinned. "That sounds like fun." She faced her daughter. "Eva?"

Eva's throat had closed. She swore she couldn't breathe. She had four weeks to persuade Alex to like her and to figure out what the hell she'd do on their wedding night.

Before she could answer, Sally said, "I'm sorry, Your Majesty, but as minister of protocol I'm in charge of the budget, so I'll need particulars on who's paying for what."

All eyes went to Karen, who looked at Eva.

Eva's heart stopped. All the blood drained from her body. "I—I mean, my mother and I—"

Alex glanced at Eva, who had gone white, and he almost cursed. She'd just told him she and her mom had no money. Her country probably had an obligation to pony up at least part of the millions it would take for a royal wedding. But with her father gone there was no one to ask. If Xaviera's legal counsel had to force Grennady to pay, the story would hit every newspaper in the world. The embarrassment of it would be horrendous for Eva.

Before he realized it, he was on his feet.

"Actually, I think we should pay for the wedding. We're the ones who called in the terms of the treaty, and said it was time for the marriage to occur." He licked his suddenly dry lips. His voice slowed as he added, "I'm just saying paying for the wedding seems like our responsibility."

Karen visibly relaxed. Eva gave him a curious look. And no wonder. He hadn't exactly ruined a way to stop this wedding, but he was participating when he should just keep his mouth shut and let it all apart.

Time slowed to a crawl.

His father cocked his head, but after only a few seconds he smiled. "You know what? He's right. We are the ones who said it was time for the marriage to take place. We'll pay for the wedding."

Sally gasped. "But, Your Majesty—"

"No buts, Sally. Alex is right."

Sally wrote something in one of her big black books. "Fine." She turned to Rose. "I'll have coffee sent to the living room where we can discuss designers."

Rose said, "Great!"

Rose and Karen began chattering about dresses, but Eva turned to Alex as he sat again. "Thanks."

He felt color rise to his cheeks. Confusion and anger with himself met and merged into an emotion that made him want to kick his own butt.

"It means nothing. The way I see it, our kingdom can absorb whatever loss results when we cancel this thing."

"Because you know my mom and I have no money."

He shrugged. "That's temporary."

She put her hand on the back of his. "Yes, but you saved us from being embarrassed."

"Is that enough to earn the payback of you backing out of the wedding?"

She laughed lightly, obviously relieved, but also the way someone would laugh with a friend. "No."

Damn her for being so cute. His mouth tugged upward until he couldn't stop a smile. "Don't make me like you."

She peeked up at him from beneath lush black eyelashes. "You'd rather hate me?"

The heat that roared through him nearly stopped his heart. Her magnetic blue-gray eyes held his. Her pretty hair rippled around an even prettier face. Everything inside of him chanted that he should lean forward and kiss her.

Kiss her.

Kiss her.
Kiss her.

But that was the real problem, wasn't it? She was pretty enough, tempting enough, that maybe she *should* be the woman he married.

And then what?

Fall in love for real?

The very thought tightened his throat. He'd loved two women in his life and lost both. Only a crazy man set himself up for that kind of pain.

"I will talk you out of this."

CHAPTER THREE

ALEX WATCHED EVA leave the dining room with her mom and Queen Rose, then exited through the hidden door in the back. Ready to change out of these stuffy clothes and put on riding breeches, he strode through the echoing maze of tall-ceilinged halls, but at his private elevator, one of his father's secretaries caught him.

The older man bowed slightly. "Your Majesty, your dad sent me to find you. He wants you in his office now."

"Now?"

The old man's eyebrows rose, an indicator Alex shouldn't argue, and that usually meant he'd done something wrong.

Alex winced. Best-case scenario was that the king wanted to chastise him for suggesting they pay for the wedding. Worst-case, he'd overheard Alex telling Eva he'd talk her out of the wedding.

Damn.

Without a word, he motioned for the man to lead him back to his father's office.

When they arrived, he entered, but the secretary reached inside to grab the doorknob, and walked out, closing the door behind him.

His father didn't look up from the letter he was signing. "You cannot talk Eva out of this wedding."

Okay. It was worst-case.

He fell to one of the velvet chairs in front of his dad's desk. "I can't believe you're forcing either of us to marry when Eva was barely out of diapers and I was pulling a wagon with my bike when that damned agreement was signed. It's ridiculous. Antiquated. And you know it."

His dad studied him for a few seconds, then he sighed heavily. "All right. You're right. And this situation is too important to leave to chance. You were smart enough to pick up on the money problem that I'd somehow missed, so I need you in the loop."

Alex sat up. "The loop?"

"Eva's dad didn't leave her mom."

"What?"

"King Mason got wind of the fact that his brother was about to stage a coup."

"So he ran?"

"For his life. His brother's coup didn't involve taking over parliament. He intended to have King Mason assassinated so he could look like a grieving brother, reluctantly filling his murdered king's shoes."

Alex sat back. "Oh, my God." He thought for a second, then said, "But if Mason dies, his brother wouldn't become king. His daughter would."

His father locked his eyes with Alex's. "Exactly."

Alex's heart thundered in his chest. "He was planning to kill Eva?"

"Gerard couldn't just murder Mason. He had to kill Eva too. The plan was to stage an accident or an attack on the palace, and have both killed at the same time, so he would be the next in line to rule. That's why we separated them. Now, the two of them dying at the same time will look like the assassination that it is."

"Oh, my God."

"This marriage isn't about a treaty. We brought Eva and her mother here on the pretense of a wedding to get them out of their palace and keep them safe."

Alex gaped in disbelief. "And you don't think putting Eva in the public eye is dangerous?"

"Exactly the opposite. As long as she's in the press, her murder would be too public. Gerard can't even do something like kidnap Eva and her mother to use as leverage to bring Mason out of hiding. It would simply call too much attention to him when he wanted all this to look like an accident."

Eva's image popped into his head. Her waist-length hair, her shy smiles, her fearless personality. The thought that someone wanted to kill her infuriated him.

"And you think a wedding keeps her safe?"

"As long as this wedding's on a fast track, Eva and her mother are protected."

Though he was angry that his father hadn't told him this in the beginning, he understood the principle behind the plan. "You're right."

The king held his gaze. "For the next four weeks, you have to cooperate. This plan only works if we can keep everybody's attention focused on a happy wedding. And that means you've got to make this look real."

Alex didn't even hesitate. "You have my word."

King Ronaldo leaned forward, laying his arms on his desk. "Once we get your wedding date announced to the press, we're off and running. That's actually why we set the date so soon. All the royal events will happen too fast and too close together for the spotlight to leave Eva. Plus, Mason doesn't believe he'll need more than four weeks to sort this out."

"What's he doing?"

"Going through back channels to figure out who he can trust, so he can get the proof he needs that his brother wanted to assassinate him. Once he gets it, he can have his brother arrested."

"He thinks his own staff is in on it?"

"Only some. But we both know it only takes trusting one wrong person to risk everything. And in this case what he risks is his life and his daughter's."

Merely thinking that someone wanted to kill Eva sent anger careening through Alex again. But he understood palace intrigue. Though there had been no siblings who wanted his father's throne, there had been other challenges. Some subtle. Some obvious. All dangerous.

"We'll do the press conference announcing your wedding tomorrow. Which means you and Eva need to be seen together this afternoon, looking like a couple getting married."

"You want us to look like we're in love?"

"No. Everybody knows you barely know each other. So I want you to look like a man and woman getting acquainted in a positive way. Then after the press conference tomorrow, you can take Eva to the country house to show her where you would live as a married couple. The press will love that. It will also keep you and Eva in the papers. And even if anyone notices the extra bodyguards, they'll just think it's because there are two of you, not you alone."

He rose. "Okay."

His father rose too. "And Alex, if Mason can't get this done in four weeks, you will be marrying her."

A wedding for a treaty was ridiculous. Marrying Eva to keep her safe gave him a weird feeling. His muscles hardened, his brain sharpened. He hardly knew the woman, but no one would hurt her on his watch.

"Absolutely."

Eva, her mom, and Queen Rose walked to the formal living room with Sally from the protocol office. Once seated on the velvet sofas, Sally ordered coffee while Eva and the dynamic mother duo got down to the business of discussing designers and considering various styles of wedding dress.

The coffee hadn't even been delivered before

a member of the palace staff arrived, whispered something to Sally and left.

Sally turned to Eva. "It seems, Princess, that Alex has arranged a date for the two of you this afternoon."

Working to keep the surprise out of her voice, she said, "He has?"

"You'll be lunching at a seaside restaurant. It will be the first time the press sees you as a couple. They won't get to ask questions, but they could shoot them at you from behind their cameras." She smiled briefly, obviously still miffed over the fact that her crown was paying for the wedding. "But you've handled this kind of thing before."

"Yes." Since she was old enough to stand behind a microphone, her dad had let her have her own voice.

She had to fight not to squeeze her eyes shut in misery. It was the first time in a week she'd had a good memory of her dad. He'd been the best supportive, funny, loving dad, and she suddenly missed him with a fierceness that brought tears to her eyes.

She blinked them away as she rose from the sofa. She refused to get maudlin over a man who had left her and her mom in such a precarious position.

"Thank you, Sally." She faced her mom and Queen Rose. "I'll need to leave to get ready."

Rose jumped up to hug her. "Enjoy the afternoon."

Karen kissed her cheek. "Yes. Enjoy yourself. Remember, brides are happy."

Rose laughed and batted her hand in dismissal. "We went through this with Ginny. Got pregnant in a one-night stand, barely knew Dom and suddenly had to marry a man she didn't know because her baby would be a king." She hugged Eva again. "It worked out for Ginny and Dom. It'll work out for you too, sugar."

"It will," Karen agreed sagely.

Eva only smiled. Obviously, they hadn't overheard any of Alex's comments about convincing her to call off the wedding.

She turned to leave, but Sally stopped her and handed her a computer tablet.

"All the links to the websites of the approved designers are in here. I'll need a name very soon so I can have him or her here ASAP to take measurements." She tapped her watch. "We don't have weeks for you to mull this over. We have, at best, a few days for you to choose a designer."

Her nerve endings popped with apprehension. Everything would be happening so fast, she had to get with the program. This afternoon's date with Alex had to be step one in her plan to get him to like her.

Three hours later, she stood in front of the mirror in her dressing room, inspecting herself. After watching several video demonstrations on flirting, she'd received a call from Alex's staff with the time and location she was to meet her betrothed.

Deciding she had a good variety of flirting techniques, she'd showered and dressed in black pants and a white top, with her long hair pinned up on her head in a tight bun.

She sighed. She looked like a librarian. Casual Prince Alex would most likely wear something übercomfortable. This outfit only highlighted their differences, all but shouting that they didn't belong together—

Oh, darn him! Now she got it. The prince who kept saying he would talk her out of this marriage hadn't scheduled this lunch as a date. He'd set it up to get them out of the palace and in front of the press, as a way to publicly demonstrate that they didn't belong together.

She fumed as the truth settled in. What better way to get her to back out of this wedding than by proving they were different? Really different. So awkward as a couple that the media might make an issue of it and make her life too miserable to endure.

Furious, she yanked the pins out of her hair and let it fall around her. She turned right, then left. The effect was better but still not good enough for the woman marrying Xaviera's casual playboy prince.

Rummaging in her drawers, she found denim capris and a flirty blue top. Sleeveless and low-cut, made of airy material that billowed out when she moved, the blouse was one of her favorites. Not only was she comfortable in it, but she was pretty. She *felt* flirty. And the videos she'd watched on YouTube said feeling flirty was half the battle. He might be on a mission to get her to dump him, but she was on the opposite mission. If it killed her, she would get him to like her enough he'd go through with this wedding.

No! By God, she would get him to fall in love with her!

After filling her black clutch bag with her phone and other necessities, she headed out.

When she saw Alex at the small side entryway where he'd indicated he would meet her, she watched his expression falter. Wearing worn boat shoes and scruffy jeans, with a white Oxford cloth shirt that tried unsuccessfully to make him respectable, he looked like a commoner. A dirt-poor, derelict commoner.

She didn't quite look that bad, but she hadn't dressed like a proper princess either, and from the quick once-over he gave her, it surprised him.

He shook his head as she approached.

She smiled. "You wanted to point out our differences by looking scruffy. But I figured out your game. So I scruffed down my outfit and, guess what? Here we are. A match."

"I did not set this up to point out our differences." He smiled engagingly. "And you'd look great no matter what you wore."

She'd look great no matter what she wore?

Eva stepped back. "What?"

"You look great. But, more important, we need to be out in public today because we'll be announcing our wedding tomorrow at a press conference."

Her eyes narrowed. "I thought you were going to talk me out of it?"

He laughed lightly. "Let's just take this one day at a time."

Her eyes narrowed even more as she studied him. He might be a nice enough guy to save her from embarrassment twice, but he did not want this wedding. He should not be acting as if everything was fine.

"All right. What's up?"

He pointed at a black Mercedes. "Nothing."

As he helped her into the car, she analyzed their situation one more time, and realized that maybe there *was* nothing wrong. He had to look attentive and proper in public or his dad would know he wasn't taking this seriously. But that really worked in her favor. She could use the four or five hours they'd spend together getting him to like her.

To her surprise, he drove, with bodyguards following them in a big black SUV. Being accustomed to security details in her own country, she didn't even blink. Instead, she glanced out the window at the scenery. Though she'd viewed most of the island from the air as her royal family's jet touched down, being close to the thick green foliage and the rocky coastline took her breath away.

She sighed.

He eyed her curiously. "What's up?"

"Your country is beautiful."

"It is."

Okay. Even though it worked in her favor, his being nice to her was getting weird.

She stole a glance at him, running the situation through her brain again. He was so sexy in his scruffy jeans and white shirt that she had to admit she sort of liked the idea of marrying him. Even if his being nice to her was an act for the press, this was her shot. Her chance. She should not be overanalyzing this. She should be using it, engaging him in normal conversation to soften him up for when she experimented with flirting.

"What was it like growing up in such a warm climate?"

He took another quick look at her. "You mean as opposed to being required to wear a parka ninety percent of the year?"

She laughed at his perceptiveness. "Yes."

"Nice." He thought for a second. "I loved the beach, but I didn't like the private area behind the palace. I wanted to be on the real beach, the public beach, with kids my own age. It wasn't easy, and my bodyguards would groan when I was home from boarding school, but they generally found a way for me to be a normal kid."

"That's why I fell in love with America. Most Europeans knew who I was. And if they didn't, they knew I was 'famous' for some reason, so they'd Google me and that would be the end of any casual relationships. But in America, even knowing I was a princess, they'd shrug and say, 'that's cool,' but otherwise, I was just a person to them."

"Interesting."

"I'm surprised you never encountered that."

He sneaked another peek at her. His brown eyes softened when he thought. His lips tilted up just slightly, as if something he remembered made him want to smile.

Tingly warmth filled her. Oh, boy. It would be so flipping easy to fall for that smile. But it wasn't real. And even though his behavior could only be an act for the press, something felt wrong. Off. Really, really off.

"Stop the car."

"What?"

She huffed out a breath. "Stop the car. Go back to the palace."

"We can't. We're supposed to be seen in public."

"I can't behave normally at a restaurant or anywhere with you acting like this. It'll make me a nervous wreck. I'll look like an idiot."

"You're fine."

"No. I'm not. And neither are you. What the hell happened to you while I was getting ready for this lunch?"

"Nothing." He laughed. "Just chill. Okay?"

"Chill?"

He shifted on his seat. "Yeah, just relax."

Her eyes narrowed. "Relax?"

"My dad wants us out there looking like people preparing to get married. So we're going out. It's nothing sinister."

"So you talked to your dad?"

He drew in a long breath as if holding back his anger—or maybe holding back a smart-assed comment, the kind of thing he would have said to her at breakfast. And her suspicions quadrupled.

"Tell me what your dad said or turn the car around. I'm not going anywhere with you until you explain yourself."

Alex realized his mistake a little too late. Of course, she was questioning his behavior. That morning he'd pushed her at breakfast then vowed to get out of marrying her. This afternoon, he was being nice to her. She was too clever not to realize something was up.

"I'm just working to keep up the pretenses for the press."

"We're in a car. No one can hear you. There's no one to be keeping up the pretense for."

"The press has extremely good long-range

camera lenses. They can pick up expressions in a car. Even a moving car."

Her eyes narrowed and she gave him that fierce silver stare of hers again.

"Which is exactly why the Alex I talked to this morning would be taking this opportunity to make us look unsuitable."

He squirmed on his seat. Damn. She was bright.

She shook her head. "Okay. Fine. You don't want to talk? Turn the car around. Take me back to the palace."

Her tirade would have been cute, except she was ruining an illusion that she desperately needed in place. He stole a peek at her with his peripheral vision. He'd never fool her for four weeks. No one would. But there was more to this than just how smart she was. This charade was life and death for her. She deserved to know the truth.

"You can't go back to the palace."

"The hell I can't!"

He sucked in a breath. "No. Really. This little tantrum you're having right now actually ruins *your* father's plan."

Her forehead wrinkled. "*My* father's plan? What does my father have to do with you suddenly being nice to me?"

"Your dad didn't leave your mom."

"Right."

"You are here, in Xaviera, because you are under my dad's protection. Your dad discovered a plot to kill him and you. The wedding is to keep you in the public eye so your uncle doesn't try to kill you or use you as leverage to bring your dad out of hiding."

She gaped at him as if only a third of what he'd said had sunk in. "What?"

"Your uncle wants to be king. But he's not getting your country's throne unless both you and your dad are out of the picture. Your dad discovered he'd hatched a plot to have both of you killed in what would look like a terrorist attack on your palace, so he left Grennady, using a cover story that seemed believable. But he's working back channels to get proof so he can have your uncle arrested."

Eva just gaped at Alex as he pulled the car into an alley and virtually hid it between two tall stucco buildings.

Killing the engine, he said, "You and I are now officially co-conspirators."

She shook her head. "This has to be a mistake."

"No. My father doesn't move on something

unless he's positive it's real." He paused, giving her a curious look. "You've never had trouble, dissension among the ranks before?"

"No." She squeezed her eyes shut.

"Xaviera's had weird things like this happen at least eight times. Last year we had a pirate who invaded our island. Dom was the one who got rid of him."

"We've never been invaded, but there's always been bad blood between my dad and his brother. They're twins. My dad was born first. Uncle Gerard has always felt two minutes cheated him out of his destiny."

"There you go."

Understanding seeped in by degrees. Her dad hadn't deserted them. But this was worse. She and her dad were in danger.

"You've got to take me back to the palace. I have to tell my mom."

"Oh, no! No. No. No. My dad took me into his confidence because he trusts me. Now I'm taking you into my confidence because this is your life we're protecting. Plus, you're too smart. At some point, maybe the wrong point, you'd have figured out something was going on behind the scenes, and if you said something, asked the wrong question at the wrong time, it would ruin everything. You need to be a part of this. Your mom doesn't."

"But she's so upset!"

"And that's what makes this plan work. As long as she's sad about your dad leaving her, but happy for you, trying to make this the best wedding ever, everybody will believe your dad left her. Besides, Rose is taking care of her."

"Does Rose know?"

He shook his head. "You, me, my dad and a very few select members of his royal guard, people who are protecting your dad and helping with his investigation."

She sank back into the comfortable leather seat.

He took her hand, kissed the knuckles. "My dad assured me your dad is safe, and that they will get to the bottom of this."

The warmth of his kiss lingered on her skin. But something more important made her smile. "You trust me."

"I guess I do. Especially since this is the first official thing my father has ever asked of me. You could make me look really, really bad if you blow this."

She glanced down at the console between them, where their joined hands sat. She'd never, ever had feelings like this before. She wasn't just making friends with this gorgeous guy. They had become partners.

"I don't want to make you look bad."

"So we've got a deal?"

She stared at their hands. His were strong and hers were tiny compared to his. They looked right together. But they weren't. This was all a ruse. A ruse to protect her life, but still a ruse.

In spite of the confusion and fear, disappointment fluttered through her. The marriage to a prince from Xaviera that she'd been dreaming about her whole life wasn't going to happen.

"Or do we not have a deal?"

Her head snapped up. She caught his gaze. She hid her disappointment that she and Alex wouldn't marry because it wasn't his fault, and he was protecting her. Her father wouldn't abdicate and she wasn't about to become a queen. She didn't have to rescue the reputation of her royal family, as she'd thought. Instead, she was protecting herself and her dad, as Alex mended his reputation with his dad—

And she could help him. She wouldn't marry him. She'd never have his children. But this fake, probably-won't-take-place marriage was more important than their real one would have ever been.

"Of course, we have a deal."

He released her hand and turned to open his car door. "Good. Let's go get some lunch and pretend we're the happiest two people in the world."

CHAPTER FOUR

"I'D LIKE TO hear how the princess feels about her dad running away with his mistress. It's only a matter of time before he abdicates his throne and then she'll be—what? The queen? Will she and Alex be moving to Grennady?"

After five minutes of talking about his engagement and taking a ribbing about finally settling down, Prince Alex wasn't surprised by the question. He also wasn't surprised when his father nudged him and Eva away from the podium and took the mic.

"You received the rules for this press conference yesterday and you know questions about the embarrassing situation with King Mason are off-limits."

Alex suppressed a smile. Leave it to his dad to tell the press what they could and couldn't ask.

"But for the record, let me state that Princess

Eva should be allowed to enjoy her engagement and wedding without being reminded that she has a father who embarrassed her family, her *country* by quite openly taking a mistress on vacation—"

"It's our understanding this woman is more than a mistress, and that King Mason left a note for his wife saying their marriage was over. If he abdicates, which a divorce will force him to do, Eva will be Grennady's new queen," a member of the press shouted from the sea of reporters below them.

Alex stole a quick glance at Karen, who straightened regally, as if to agree with his father. The actions of her husband would not put a damper on her daughter's wedding.

King Ronaldo's eyebrows rose. "I said no questions or comments about this and I meant that. This wedding is a happy occasion and I intend to keep it that way."

"But he's—"

That was all Alex heard before being whisked out of the press room, Eva at his side.

In the hall outside the press room, his father straightened regally. "All things considered, I'd say that went very well."

Eva nodded. "Yes. Thank you."

Her congenial reply made the king's expression go from proud to confused. Alex could almost see the wheels turning in his head as he realized she knew enough about the situation to thank him. And there was only one way she could know.

The king snapped his gaze to Alex's.

Alex inclined his head toward Eva, a silent indicator that he'd told her. His father hadn't said he couldn't, though it was clear he'd counted on Alex's discretion. But, in his opinion, Eva didn't just have a right to know; Alex had had a responsibility to tell her.

Getting the message, his father sighed. "Okay, then. I hope you two know what you're doing."

Alex said, "We do," at the same time that Eva said, "We do."

Alex stole a glance at her. He wouldn't exactly call her stubborn but she was her own woman. A woman, the comment from the press had reminded all of them, who would someday be a queen.

Still, she was in line for the throne of a rather young king. Her dad wasn't even fifty yet. Plus, most kings didn't retire. Mason could rule until the day he died. But if Eva's dad died unexpectedly or decided to retire, she would be queen of her own country.

After only a few days with her, he could see it. He could envision her overseeing a parliament, directing the affairs of a country.

Obviously not pleased, but resigned to their situation, King Ronaldo sighed and walked away.

Chatting about the imminent arrival of the designer who had been chosen for Eva's dress, Queen Rose and Karen also walked away.

With a quick kiss on Ginny's cheek, Dom headed for his office, and Ginny excused herself to go to her apartment to check on the baby.

Alex directed Eva to the right, toward the elevator that would take them to the floor for her apartment.

Eva quietly said, "Your dad is very clever."

He laughed. "No kidding. It's one of the reasons Dom works so hard. He's got very big shoes to fill." He stopped talking, waiting for the elevator to reach them. When they were inside, behind the closed door where no one could overhear, he stole a glance at her.

"I know your dad isn't abdicating and you're not going to be taking your throne in the immediate future, but that doesn't change the fact that you'll someday be a queen."

She straightened, the same way his father

did, and Alex laughed again. "Oh, yeah. You've thought about it."

"Actually, my father and I have discussed it. When Dom married Ginny my dad told me it was a blessing because my entire focus was needed to be Queen of Grennady. And I probably will be for a while. But, honestly, I don't think I'm made to rule."

"Oh, trust me. You are."

"I hope to be in my sixties before my father dies. Which could make my oldest son close to forty. And ready to reign. I see myself more in the role of placeholder for a few years to soften the blow of my father's death, then I'll turn everything over to him."

He tilted his head and studied her. "You really have thought it all through."

"Of course I have. Ruling lines don't think in terms of decades. We think in terms of generations. But you know that."

He shrugged. "Sort of."

"Which was why I didn't argue this marriage. I know your bloodline. I know you and I would have produced a wonderful king."

He shook his head. "My son would have been a king."

She stepped close, straightened the collar of

his shirt and then his tie. "Does it make you sorry you're not marrying me?"

He looked down, into her pretty gray-blue eyes and at her smiling face. He let his gaze skim her soft black hair. When his gaze fell to her lips, the one kiss they'd shared jumped into his brain. That one really hot, really great kiss.

For a second he almost was sorry he wasn't marrying her, but not for the reasons she thought.

The elevator door opened. He ignored it. "If your dad doesn't straighten things out before our wedding date, we may still be getting married."

"Let's hope it doesn't come to that. But even if it does, we can get an annulment. Far different than a divorce. It won't preclude me from taking the throne."

She took a step to walk out of the elevator, but he caught her hand, stopping her and letting the door close behind her. Trapped in the gaze of her magnetic blue eyes, he saw some problems she didn't. She talked about this wedding as if it were nothing but a business deal, but he could see a million reasons she could get sucked into it.

"I just don't want you to get any ideas while we spend four weeks together."

She laughed. "I liked it better when you kissed me to warn me off."

More memories of the kiss flooded him. And here she was again, within reach, working her smart mouth against him, filling him with challenge.

She smiled, put her small white hand on his chest. "Maybe you're warning me because you need the warning yourself."

The elevator door opened again. This time, he let her walk out, but he called after her, "Be ready at four. I'm to take you to the country house to show you where we'll be living."

She turned, smiled and nodded, then walked away.

Alex sucked in a steadying breath. Her behavior should infuriate him. Instead, it constantly challenged him. What would it be like to be the guy who tamed a future queen? She might be the woman who ruled their country, but he would be the guy who ruled their bed.

He shook his head to dislodge that thought before it took root. He wasn't marrying anyone ever. Let alone someone who would be his ruler.

* * *

Eva managed to remain perfectly cool until she was behind the door of her apartment. Then she leaned against it and squeezed her eyes shut.

Why in the hell had she just flirted with him?

She shook her head on the way to her bedroom. Of all the times for those stupid flirting videos she'd watched on YouTube to pop into her head, the day after he'd told her the truth about their marriage was the worst.

Still, he'd presented her with eight or ten really good jumping-off points, and in the end she couldn't fight her brain from using the knowledge it now had—

Oh, please. If there was one thing Eva didn't do it was kid herself, and she wouldn't let herself start now. She'd flirted because she'd wanted to. The Alex she'd met at the stables had been angry. The Alex she'd dealt with at her arrival dinner and breakfast the morning they'd chosen the wedding date had been determined to talk her out of it. The Alex who'd been released from his commitment was fun. Happy-go-lucky. Yet fiercely determined to protect her and her dad. His brown eyes sparked with the challenge of their situation.

He clearly liked having a role, a part to play, and he was a natural.

Plus, he looked great in a suit. Really handsome.

Put all that together and the man was just sexy.

Tempting.

And oh, so easy to tease.

She told herself to stop thinking like that. Not because she was worried for her life. She wasn't. She trusted King Ronaldo and Xaviera's royal guard to keep her safe. And she trusted her dad to find the proof, arrest his brother and right their world.

The problem was, at any time before the wedding her dad could call and say he had everything in hand and she and her mom could go home. This might go the whole way to the day before the wedding or it could end tomorrow, but no matter how long the ruse lasted, she would be going home. Without Alex.

Getting involved with him was pointless. Except—

As Alex had reminded her, she was also a woman who would be a queen, who had to produce a royal heir, who had no skills with men.

She might not be marrying Prince Alex Sancho, but her four weeks with him could help her figure out how she could find the husband she'd need to do her duty and create an heir.

Alex had just reached his apartment door when his cell phone buzzed with a text. He pulled his phone from his pocket and saw the message from Dom.

Meet me in your office.

He almost laughed. He hadn't been in his own office in months. Meetings were typically held in the king's office or Dom's. He didn't exactly have a lot of official business.

Still…

It felt right. Maybe because his father had taken him into his confidence about Eva's situation, but he suddenly didn't mind being called to his office.

He typed, On my way… turned around and took his elevator back to the first floor.

Dom awaited him in the empty secretary's space that fronted his furnished, but never used office. "Hey, kid."

"Hey, older brother." He led Dom into the room, walked behind his desk and fell to the chair that was slightly uncomfortable, given that no one had worn it in. The walls were paneled with rich wood. Thick Persian rugs covered the floors. Velvet drapes framed the huge window that overlooked the courtyard. And no one ever saw any of it.

Dom sat on one of the chairs in front of his desk. "Dad told me about King Mason."

"He did?"

"Yes. After your talk with him, he realized it wasn't right that he was doing an end run around me with the royal guard I supervise."

"Wow. He's really loosening up."

Dominic chuckled. "Dad's not the hard case you think he is. In the past months, he's been handing over a lot of his responsibilities to me." He caught Alex's gaze. "And he sees you as the one running point on this situation with Eva and her mom."

"Running point?" He sniffed, not quite sure how to handle the fact that his father trusted him. "For the next four weeks I'm going to be dating a really pretty girl."

Dom laughed. "That's one way to look at it. Or you could say that for the next four weeks you're protecting the daughter of one of Dad's closest political allies. It's a big deal."

Alex rolled his eyes. "I was making a joke."

"Right. You love being funny. But you're ready for this. As much as you like pretending that you aren't." He shifted on his seat. "I took a few minutes to go over everything that happened at the press conference and you and Eva were great."

Alex laughed. "We're both born to this life. We know how to keep up appearances."

"And you did. But here's the thing. The two of you stood close together at the podium. You smiled at each other at just the right times. But when we left the press room and gathered in the hall, your demeanors changed. There was a visible distance between you."

"So? The press couldn't see."

"I know, but the biggest group of people you have to fool wasn't in that press room. They were in the corridor outside the press room."

Alex frowned.

"It's our staff. It took only two phone calls for my secretary to get the scoop that you've never been to Eva's apartment and she's never been to yours."

Alex's face scrunched in disbelief. "What?"

"The staff knows you've basically just met, so it's not like they expect you to be sleeping together, but they're gossiping about the fact that the only times you're seen together are when you're expected to be."

"Really?"

"There's a betting pool. All the stable boys believe you'll never actually marry. The maids are divided. And even though Chef's a romantic she's betting against the marriage too. That's not good for your charade."

He sat up, totally confused by the fact that he hadn't thought of this. "I guess not."

Dom rose. "Convincing the staff here at the palace should be your first priority. In fact, if I were you, I'd put on such a show that the stable boys start changing their bets and the maids can't resist gossiping to their neighbors."

Alex leaned back in his chair. He appreciated the heads-up. He would have figured it out for himself in another day or two, but he was glad he hadn't had to.

He pulled his phone out of his pocket and brought his schedule onto the screen. He cancelled every event he had arranged for the next week.

He glanced up at Dom. "If you don't mind, I'd like to see any plans the guard put in place for Eva's protection, and the names of the men in her security details."

"I'll tell the lieutenant."

Alex rose. "Great."

As Dom turned to the door, he said, "And don't forget what I told you about the staff."

"I won't."

After Dom left, Alex thought for another second, then strode out of the office.

The staff hadn't seen him in Eva's apartment? Well, there was no better time than the present. He took the elevator to the guest floor, walked down the massive hall to her rooms and lifted his hand to knock—

A fiancé wouldn't knock.

He opened the door and ambled through the tall-ceilinged foyer to the living room.

"Alex!" his stepmother yelped as she tossed a white robe to Eva who stood on a platform similar to the one his tailor used. She hugged the robe to her bosom, but it was too late. He'd seen the yellow bra and panties. He'd seen the creamy white arc of her breasts. He'd seen the curve of her hip.

He stopped dead in his tracks.

Rose about had a coronary. "What are you doing here? And why didn't you knock?"

"A fiancé doesn't knock." He tried not to watch as Eva turned her back to him and slipped into the robe. But the vision from the back was as awe-inspiring as the front. For a short woman, she had a long, sloping back that ended in perfect round hips and a round butt.

Eva slid into the robe, yanked the belt at her

waist and turned to the sixty-something man who stood with a tape measure in hand, gaping at Alex.

"Could you give us a minute?"

The older man said, "Of course, but only a minute. Considering time for fittings, I've got about two weeks to make a gown the whole world is going to see. Everybody's got to be on board with the timing or I swear I will fold like a house of cards."

Composed now, Rose took his arm. "Of course, we'll cooperate with your timing." She tossed Alex a pointed look. "This will not happen again."

"At least not without a phone call to warn us you're coming," Eva's mom said haughtily. "You might be engaged, but a gentleman caller is still a gentleman caller."

The three trooped out of the room and Alex laughed. "Have a lot of gentleman callers, do you?"

"My mom is struggling to find any sense of normalcy in this situation. She thinks her husband left her. And she's in the public eye. If she wants to ban you from the room, I say we let her."

"We can't. Dom reminded me this morning

that the most important group we have to fool is the servants."

She frowned.

"The palace staff. There's a betting pool. Apparently no one believes I'll actually marry you."

Her delicate eyebrows rose. "And who do we have to thank for that, Mr. Date-Every-Woman-in-the-Known-Universe?"

"You're a woman in the known universe and I never dated you."

She held up one finger to stop him. "No, you haven't. And maybe that's the problem. Just jumping into this wedding the way we have, everybody sees it as nothing but a royal responsibility." She tapped her finger against her lips, thinking. "So maybe what we need to do is have a date. A real date. Not lunch, but something smashing."

"In front of the staff," Alex reminded her, letting his gaze roam along her fluffy white robe, knowing the pretty bra and panties were beneath, and that they covered a gorgeous butt and breasts just the right size for his hands. "That means the trip to the country home is cancelled. It smacks of PR."

"So what can we do here? In the palace?"

He knew one very important thing they

could do. In his apartment. In his bedroom. Too bad the staff couldn't see that. But they would see the seduction leading up to it—

"Have dinner at my apartment."

She laughed. "Oh, how many times have you used that line?"

The way she said it cut through him like a knife. His success with women was legendary. But in a good way. She didn't have to sound so snooty about it. "I wasn't that bad."

She stepped down from the platform, tightened the belt with a quick yank. "Oh, please."

"You know, maybe we're looking at this all wrong. Maybe the reason the staff doesn't think the wedding will come off is you?"

She gasped. "Me?"

"You have an attitude about me."

She gaped at him.

"Maybe what you need to do is start being nicer to me."

"Okay. Fine. I'll be nicer to you. But I need specifics so I can do some prep work. What's your plan for tonight?"

"If this was a normal date, I'd call the kitchen staff and tell them to set up a romantic dinner around eight. You'd arrive in something pretty and I'd be spellbindingly witty while they served dinner. We'd dismiss them after they served the main course. Then you'd still be at my apartment tomorrow when they bring up breakfast, and it would look like things got so cozy that you didn't leave."

Eva swallowed. She could picture it. She'd be wearing a pretty gown; he'd be in a tux. She'd be shy. He'd be…well, himself. Playful. Sexy. Seductive.

She swallowed again. "It works." She cleared her throat. It really, really worked. She got breathless just imagining it. Plus, four hours of a dinner with him, while he was being himself? Just think of the flirting practice she'd get.

Queen Rose walked into the living room again. "We have a designer who's about to melt into a puddle of despair if we don't get your measurements today. Can we speed this up?"

Eva said, "Yes, of course. Give us one more minute." She faced Alex. "I'll be there at eight."

Alex smiled. "And take a nap. I don't want the serving staff telling the press you yawned all night. I want them thinking all kinds of naughty thoughts when they find your gown on the floor."

"My gown on the floor?" Her face turned

red, but she understood what he was saying. There was no better way to perpetuate a story than to physically stage it. "Okay."

"Maybe we'll make a whole trail. Gown. Bra. Panties…" He caught her gaze. "My shirt."

Picturing undressing in front of him and having him take his shirt off in front of her sent her hormones scrambling.

He leaned toward her and kissed her cheek. "This'll be fun."

CHAPTER FIVE

WHEN HIS DOORBELL rang at eight, Alex walked through the foyer entryway to answer it. He straightened the bow tie of his tux, before reaching down for the knob to open the door for her.

"Good—"

His voice faltered when he saw her in a yellow gown, the same color as the bra and panties she'd been wearing when he accidentally walked in on her fitting. For a good twenty seconds, he was struck dumb. Then common sense filtered through the image of her standing on the tailor's platform. Yes, he'd seen her in a bra and panties, but he'd seen women dressed in far less at the beach.

"—evening."

He sucked in a breath. He might have seen women dressed in less, but that didn't take away from the fact that she was beautiful. Her dark hair had been pulled up in a style that reminded him of a Greek goddess. Her dress clung to her curves, but just at the bottom of her hip it flared into tons of material that frothed out like a bell. "You look amazing."

She smiled. "Thanks."

Her humble acceptance of his compliment did crazy things to his pulse, but he didn't try to pretend he didn't know why. Her innocence struck a funny chord with him. And why not? Her naiveté made her sweet. It had been a long time since he'd met, let alone spent time with, a woman who was sweet.

But she was also strong. Pretty much his smart-ass equal when he pushed her, which made her kind of fun to be with. He'd have to be deaf, dumb and blind not to be attracted to her.

But that might be good. What better way to get the tongues of the staff wagging than to let himself act naturally, the way he would with any beautiful woman?

He reached down, took her hand and kissed the palm. "I hope you like Italian."

He saw the little pulse point at her throat jump. Too bad the servants hadn't seen that.

She laughed nervously. "Something rich and fattening?"

"Of course. I'm sure we can find a way to work off the calories."

He'd said that for the benefit of the young man who'd walked to the table set up by the large window to light the candles, but Eva's nervous laugh returned.

He smiled. After his thirty-second lapse of sanity after seeing her in the dress the same color as her panties and bra that afternoon, it was good to knock her off balance, too. They had to appear to be attracted to each other. Not just him to be tongue-tied over her. They also needed for her to be smitten around him.

Still holding her hand, he led her into the living room where two glasses of wine sat on the low table in front of the sofa.

"I took the liberty of choosing a wine."

She smiled and accepted the glass from him. This smile wasn't nervous, but pretty. Soft. Sensual.

His attraction returned—expanded—became more of an urge for action than a feeling. He pictured himself running his hands along her curved torso, and the lines between reality and pretense blurred a bit. If he'd met her in a casino he would have pursued an evening like this for real. She was pretty. Her innocence was endearing. And she made him work for her affection. If nothing else, the challenge of it appealed to him.

But this wasn't real. It was a fiction for the benefit of the press. He was supposed to be acting. Playing a part. He shouldn't be having real urges.

He directed her to the sofa. They sat together, side by side, and the soft material of her gown billowed around her as if she were buried in fabric. But, really, no matter how huge the skirt, a strapless gown was only held together by a hook-and-eye catch and a very long zipper. He could probably have that gown undone in twenty seconds, and then he'd get to touch all that soft-looking skin.

Damn it! What the hell was wrong with him? This was supposed to be acting, not fantasizing.

He stretched out the collar beneath his bow tie. "Is it warm in here?"

She fanned herself. "A little."

"Maybe we should just get right to dinner?"

She rose. "I am hungry."

"Good." He set his hand on the small of her back, directing her to the table set up by a wall of windows that displayed the sea behind the palace.

After he pulled out her chair, she sat and looked up at him with a smile. "What an amazing view! This is lovely."

He stared down at her. When she was re-laxed, her eyes were a soft, pretty blue. He liked it almost as much as the sharp color they turned when she was angry or determined.

Realizing he was doing it again—behav-ing as if this was real—he jumped away from her, tugged the vest of his tux into place and walked to his seat across from her.

"Thank you. Our legend is that it took three years to build our palace."

She opened her napkin and set it on her lap as servants began bringing salads. "I'd love to hear about it."

He shrugged, feeling awkward. This scene should have been a piece of cake for him. But once again urges and possibilities flashed through his mind. Things he could do. Things he'd like to do. Things he knew he wasn't sup-posed to do. Because this was a charade.

It was crazy. Odd. Confusing.

"There's not much to tell. It took my ances-tors three years to build this back in the Mid-dle Ages. End of story."

"But it's so modern."

He cautiously met her gaze. "We've added on."

"And done a lovely job."

The servants stepped back, but they didn't

leave. He and Eva began eating their salads. The room was quiet, as if populated by two people with nothing to say. Which was ridiculous. He was a pro. He'd had a thousand first dates. Hundreds of dates in this apartment. And he knew the goal. It wasn't to take her to bed or even kiss her. This was all about fooling the servants. They had to jump to conclusions when they found her dress on the floor the next morning. And they wouldn't, if he couldn't even talk to her.

He cleared his throat. "And what about your palace?"

"It's a little cozier."

"You mean smaller."

"No. I mean cozier. There's a fireplace in every room. There are only a few months in the year when we don't need a fire. We wear warm pajamas and do a lot of snuggling."

He laughed, but he suddenly pictured her in flannel PJs, sitting under a warm blanket, in front of a fire. She was curvy and soft. Made for snuggling. Made for fires and cognac.

Damn it. Why was he doing this?

"Tell me about your education." The sentence wasn't fully out of his mouth before he winced. He wanted the servers to run to the press with stories of red-hot kisses, not two people reading their biographies.

He had to get his head in the game. He was sharper than this.

"Are you okay?"

He laughed and combed his fingers through his hair. "I'm fine."

But they ate most of the dinner in silence because he couldn't think of anything to say. Every time he came up with something suitable, something intimate, it wouldn't feel like part of a ruse. It would feel real, so real, his nerves tingled with an anticipation he wasn't allowed to feel.

When the meal was eaten, he escorted her to the sofa, and walked to the bar. "What can I get you?"

"Why don't we just stick with wine?"

"Great idea."

"Good."

She smiled the soft smile and he fought an avalanche of urges. The urge to tease her. The urge to tell her just how great she looked in yellow. The urge to make short order of her gown and slide his hands along the curve of her waist...

But every time he decided it was okay to make an urge a reality, as part of the ruse, his stomach tumbled. Kisses that were meant to be seen by the staff weren't supposed to have actual meaning. Even she'd believe they were fake. But he really wanted this.

Which was wrong for so many different reasons he couldn't even count them.

He poured more wine and sat beside her on the sofa.

"I don't think it's inappropriate for us to talk about our pasts."

He glanced around, saw no one was listening and said, "Except we're getting married. We should already know each other's pasts."

"Not really. It's an arranged marriage. Besides, I once heard that the best way to get people to believe a lie is to stick with the truth as much as possible."

He laughed at the wonderfully naive way she said that. "Who told you that?"

"A vet who came to the shelter. She was one of those people who talked all the time." She laughed. "Knew a little something about everything." She tilted her head. "Not sure why I suddenly remembered that."

"Because we need it?"

"Maybe. But I think the real problem is you know a great deal about me, but I know very little about you beyond the stuff everybody sees: the fact that you date a lot, love casinos and in general goof off."

"Because that's about all there is."

"Really? That's it? You've never been in love?"

The question hit him like a sucker punch. He should have expected it, but hadn't, and when Nina's face popped into his head, it threw him for a loop.

He pulled in a quiet breath.

She leaned in. "It would make the charade so much more believable if the staff heard you telling me the truth."

Realizing his reaction had given him away, he raised his gaze, met her pretty blue eyes. "Yes. I was in love. Once."

"What happened?"

He said, "She left me," because that was the easy, no-explanation-necessary way of telling the story. But when he said it, his chest tightened and his brain froze.

"Why did she leave you?"

He swallowed.

Her gaze swept his face. "She must have broken your heart."

The vise grip on his chest tightened another notch. His brain jumped in revolt at the way he was fooling her, even though this wasn't the first time he'd used this loophole in his explanation. He'd never really admitted the truth in his Nina story to anyone. Yet, he knew if he wasn't totally honest, Eva's questions would continue. The conclusions she'd draw would be wrong.

"She died."

Eva pressed her hand to her chest. "Oh. I'm so sorry."

His mouth felt dry. Dusty. He took a sip of wine.

She said, "I'm sorry," again. "Really, we can talk about something else."

But he pictured Nina, always in a bikini, always on a boat or a Jet Ski or water skis.

He swiped his hand across his mouth. "Yeah, we should probably talk about something else."

"Sure."

The room got quiet. Except for the sounds of the staff gathering dishes and silverware from the table by the window, his entire apartment was silent.

"Was she pretty?"

He blew out his breath. "That's not talking about something else."

"I know."

She smiled, and for the second time in only a few minutes he got the sucker punch. Resisting that smile would be harder than telling a few simple, unemotional facts.

"She was very pretty. Tall, blonde, and only twenty-two." He shrugged. "Of course, I wasn't much older."

"So it was a long time ago?"

"Five years."

"You're past it, then?"

He should be. Most days he thought he was.

"Did your father like her?"

That made him laugh. "We spent most of our time on the water. Jet Skis. Water skiing. Diving. Because all that kept me out of the casinos, my father thought she was good for me."

Eva eased back on the sofa, getting comfortable. Alex leaned back too. They sat side by side. With only a slight tilt of their heads, they could look at the ceiling.

"*Was* she good for you?"

Alex shrugged. "We were daredevils." And things he hadn't thought about in those five years began tiptoeing into his brain. "There was no official investigation into her accident, or if there had been her father kept it hushed up. But I heard from the people with her that day that she'd been driving too fast, pushing boundaries."

"I'm sorry."

He sniffed. "It's not your fault. If anything, it was hers." Saying the words out loud hurt his chest. Crumbled his heart into a thousand pieces. Until this very moment, he hadn't realized how angry he was with Nina. "And now it's officially time to talk about something else."

"Want to hear about the guy who almost had me calling my parents to see if I could get out of my marriage to Dominic?"

He laughed with relief. "Absolutely."

"It was my first year at university. He was a tremendous geek."

He laughed again, thinking it remarkable that he could talk so openly about Nina, then two seconds later laugh.

"A geek?"

"Oh, I thought he was so brilliant. I hung on his every word."

"I'm not exactly brilliant."

She turned her head on the sofa and waited until he turned his, and their eyes met. "I'm not exactly the water skiing type. I've never water skied. I'm not fond of boats. *Daredevil* is the last word anyone would use to describe me."

Yet right at that moment he wanted to kiss her more than he wanted his next breath of air. His body tingled when she was around. She made him laugh. Protecting her gave him a great sense of responsibility that didn't annoy him, it pleased him. And he'd told her about Nina.

Oh, no.

He was beginning to like her. For real. That's why seeing her in the bra and panties had switched him into genuine seduction mode. Getting feelings for her brought reality into their fantasy.

He bounced up on the sofa, noticed the last servant leaving the dining area by the window, and reached down for her hand to help her stand. "Well, that was certainly an interesting conversation, but all the servants are in the kitchen now. In five minutes everybody will be out of here."

She glanced at his hand. Her head tilted in confusion.

"You can take off your dress—" in the bathroom, behind closed doors so he didn't see "—and be on your way."

She frowned. "That's it?"

"What did you think? This is a charade." Stronger now that he'd figured out why he felt so different around her tonight, he caught her gaze. "We're not really going to sleep together."

But his heart felt funny as the words slid out of his mouth.

When she finally took his hand and said, "No. I'm sorry. I just somehow thought I'd be staying longer," his heart squeezed.

He stepped back. He wasn't letting one slip-up cloud his brain. So he liked her? He liked a lot of women. This was a charade. To protect her. He couldn't—wouldn't—let these feelings for her grow.

He shifted another step away from her. "No point in going overboard."

Especially since these feelings were amazingly different. Warm. Happy. The kind of feelings he'd run from his entire life.

CHAPTER SIX

ALEX DIRECTED HER to a powder room, where she removed her gown and slipped into the sundress she'd squished into her little clutch purse. She walked out, handed her gown to him and watched him drop it to the floor about halfway down a discreet hallway. Then he walked her to a back door.

He motioned for her to go before him into a thin, quiet hall. "This corridor is private. Even servants aren't allowed to use it."

They reached the elevator and he pressed the button. The doors opened.

She waited a beat. Not quite sure what she wanted until she realized she was waiting for him to kiss her good-night—though she wasn't quite sure why. This was a ruse with a purpose. Not real. The only time they had to pretend they liked each other was when someone was watching. And no one was watching—

Hadn't he reminded her of that?

He stepped back. His hand on the elevator door, holding it open, but now a good two feet away from her, he said, "Good night."

Disappointment fluttered through her. "Good night."

She stepped into the elevator, believing herself certifiable. Why the hell would she possibly have stood there like a ninny expecting him to kiss her…?

Because she'd seen the odd looks he'd given her, caught him staring at her face and gazing into her eyes, and knew he was beginning to like her.

Still, only an idiot would have missed how he'd changed when he started talking about the woman he'd loved. The one who had died.

As the elevator rose to her floor, her heart caught a bit at the thought of his loss. She'd never lost anyone. Never really had her heart broken, but he had. He hadn't just lost his first love. His mother had died. He'd been through things she'd never even considered. It was no wonder he lived a surface life. Hid his feelings. Tried to pretend he didn't have feelings. He was protecting himself.

She couldn't fault him for that, even if it did disappoint her that he'd rushed her out, and hadn't made good on the promise that they'd make a trail of clothes.

She almost giggled at the devilishness of that, but caught herself. He wouldn't have swooned at the sight of her stripping. Though she couldn't say the same for watching him take off his shirt—

The elevator arrived at her floor and she sighed. Why was she thinking like this?

Because he was good-looking.

Because he was smart.

Because he trusted her enough to tell her about her dad, to make her a co-conspirator.

And tonight he'd told her about his lost love.

The few days they'd spent together they'd been forced to be brutally honest. She hadn't just been honest with him; he'd been honest with her. And, God help her, she'd liked it.

Like it? Or liked him?

She squeezed her eyes shut. She didn't know. But the evening had been different than she'd expected. Very different. Instead of struggling to keep her dignity while he tried to impress the servants with his sexual prowess, they'd talked.

And it had been nice.

No, better than nice. It had been one of the best nights of her life.

She shook her head as a crazy thought filled it.

What if pretending to be involved, being co-conspirators, put them in each other's company enough that they actually grew to like each other?

He was confiding in her. She was relaxing with him. Was it so far-fetched to think that a charade actually set them up to fall in love?

It might not be far-fetched but it did sound a hell of a lot like wishful thinking. Especially since a few short days before they'd been at odds.

Still, when she went to bed that night, she thought of telling him that her palace was cozy and she smiled. She wouldn't mind sitting in front of a fire with him.

The next day Eva had breakfast with her mom, and spent the morning with her and Queen Rose, looking at table arrangements for the engagement party to be held in less than two weeks and the wedding two weeks after that. When Alex called and told her they would be going to dinner that night, both mothers made kissing noises.

Remembering that they believed this wedding was real, she blushed. They thought it was cute, but actually it was lying to her mom that embarrassed her. Still, it was for a good cause. And any day now her mom would know that.

And any day now, she and Alex wouldn't be in this game they were playing out to help her dad. That was probably the best reason to keep her wits about her. They didn't have the four weeks everybody thought they did. Her dad could call tomorrow, and they'd never see each other again.

When Alex came to her apartment to pick her up, he immediately glanced around to see if anyone was there.

"Mom is having dinner with your dad and stepmom."

He visibly relaxed. "Good. Because I wanted to apologize for being abrupt last night."

She said, "That's okay." Then after a slight pause, she carefully added, "I was kind of glad you shared." She didn't want to make a big deal out of it. She especially didn't want to say so much that he'd realize she was getting feelings for him. The man was a playboy. And she was someday going to be a queen. She couldn't be falling for a guy who would very publicly break her heart. But she did need to acknowledge the obvious. They'd shared some secrets.

"Nina died five years ago. I'm over it."

"I get that. I still appreciate that you told me."

He mumbled something under his breath, walked over to the door and opened it for her.

"I'll tell you what. We'll put the top down on the Mercedes." He dangled his car keys. "And I'll even let you drive, if you promise to forget I told you any of that."

Walking to the door, she snatched the keys out of his hand. This was what they did best. Argue. Playfully, of course. She finally figured out that was the way he liked life, conversations, maybe even relationships. Easy. Silly. Meaningless.

"Oops. Looks like you just lost your leverage."

He laughed but didn't try to take the keys back. Once she settled in behind the steering wheel of his car, she started the engine and Alex pressed the button that folded the roof down.

She breathed in the warm Xaviera air. "I'm gonna miss this."

He laughed. "I thought you liked being snuggled in front of fireplaces."

She waved to the bodyguards, put the gear-shift into Drive and drove to the gate which opened in front of her, then off palace grounds. The air was warm and sweet, and the way Alex remembered that detail of her life made her feel soft and squishy inside.

But she didn't say anything.

"No comment on the fact that I remembered your palace is cozy?"

"No." She stole a peek at him. "That would sort of be like flirting." And what a hell of a time for her to finally catch on. "If we were in public where the press could overhear, I might have said how nice it was you remembered, and maybe tease you into admitting you'd like to sit with me under a blanket in front of the fire. Where we could, you know, snuggle up and *accidentally* rub up against each other. But since we're alone there's no point."

She glanced over at him again. His eyes were wide. His mouth was sort of open.

"What?" She shook her head. "The whole flirting thing is new to me. I got that wrong, didn't I?"

"No. No. You were fine."

"The part about rubbing up against each other under the blanket... That was too much?"

"Nope. That was pretty much spot-on. Class-A flirting."

She cast a quick look at him, knowing she was grinning like an idiot. "So I'm getting it?"

"You never tried to flirt with the geek?" Before she could answer, he shook his head. "No. Of course, you didn't. You probably were like a deer in the headlights around him."

She laughed and attraction sharpened all of Alex's senses, but he ignored it. He'd sorted all this out the night before. He could not fall for her. He was not the kind of guy who had relationships. It was best to just do what he needed to do, but otherwise maintain his distance.

The best way to do that would be to keep them both busy. So he took her to a casino after dinner, and showed her how to play blackjack. She wore a pale pink gown that made her look sweet and innocent. Her long black ponytail heightened the effect, and he was glad. She was tempting, but also innocent, and the visual reminder that he could hurt her if he acted on his impulses got his head in the game.

The dealer dealt her an ace, then gave a card to the other four players at their half circle table. When he came back to Eva, Alex said, "Take a card."

She sat and he stood behind her. He'd had to lean down to look at her card. But that was okay. He could smell her perfume, feel the smoothness of her shoulder as he brushed it, but he was in control now.

She peeked up at him. "Take a card?"

"Say hit me."

She laughed. "I've never before asked to be hit."

In the few days he'd spent in her company, he knew there were a million things she'd never done. A million things he'd love to show her.

He kept all that to himself. "So, go ahead. Say it."

With a giggle, she faced the dealer. "Hit me."

The dealer laughed too as he pulled a card from the dispenser. "Ten." He met Eva's gaze. "Twenty-one."

She peeked back at Alex.

"You win."

She jumped off her seat. "I win!" She spun to face Alex. "I win!" Like Rose on steroids, she enveloped him in a fast hug. But when she pulled away, their gazes caught, and he could see in her shiny silver-blue orbs the very second she realized she had her hands wrapped around his biceps.

Time stopped.

They stared into each other's eyes, both of

them silently acknowledging that having her hands on him felt good.

But she didn't step back, didn't pull away. She just kept gazing into his eyes, as if spellbound.

And he wanted to curse. The innocence that was so tempting was the very thing that would keep her safe from him. Yet tonight he wanted to be with her. To just let his guard down and see where the night would take them.

But he wouldn't do that. No matter how much he thought he wanted her tonight, they potentially had weeks of being together. He would not make this into something it wasn't supposed to be. Something that might hurt her.

He plucked her hands off his arms and directed her back to her seat. "All right, Cinderella. That was just your first hand. You've got a whole night ahead of you."

She laughed but there was a hesitancy to it. What passed between them had been a powerful, but normal, male/female thing, yet it had thrown her for a loop.

The odd protective feeling he felt around her grew, swelling into something that had him looking around. There were three bodyguards playing blackjack at the surrounding tables. He knew there were another six or so at the casino entrances and stationed strategically nearby. But anxiety caused his nerve endings to jump.

He pulled back from Eva and casually motioned to his lead guard. When he came over, Alex whispered, "Do we have a female guard?"

"No, Your Majesty."

"It's something we might want to consider for tomorrow."

When the guard frowned, he whispered, "For the ladies' room and other places she goes that we can't go."

He looked around the casino floor and saw more flaws in the security. Not because his team was inept but because he'd decided on a whim to teach her how to play blackjack, and his people weren't as prepared as they normally would have been.

"We'll need a meeting tomorrow morning."

The guard bowed. "Yes, Your Majesty."

A few days later, the rumor finally got out that housekeeping had found Eva's gown on the floor of the hallway leading to Alex's bedroom. A firestorm erupted in the tabloids. Alex couldn't take Eva to lunch without reporters shouting questions at them. From that day forward, they never went anywhere without a plan.

After every outing Alex held a debriefing. His father and Dom attended the first meeting. Dom was still in attendance after the third. But four days in, Alex was handling Eva's security on his own.

And rightly so. Because he was with Eva everywhere she went, he considered himself to be her number one bodyguard. Her first line of defense. No one questioned why he stood so close or held her hand every time they walked. He was her fiancé. But really, he was watching, waiting, ready to stand in front of her or pull her out of the way if anything happened.

Two days before their engagement party, he automatically caught her hand as they walked out of the casino at the end of their evening together. Night air warmed them as his limo driver strode around the hood of the vehicle to open the door for them.

Before they could get into the car, a guy in jeans and a big T-shirt with a camera strapped around his neck ambled up to them. "You know it's funny. I've never seen you steal a kiss."

Alex's bodyguards instantly tensed. But Alex smiled. He'd seen this kid in press conferences and knew he was credentialed, not a threat.

"Did you ever stop to think that there's a reason for that."

The guy laughed. "Yeah. You've never kissed her."

"He's kissed me," Eva said, then she blushed, and Alex felt his own color rise. Not because he was embarrassed but because that kiss had been such a scorcher. With his mind wrapped up in her security, he'd forgotten that kiss. But the reminder brought all his feelings back to life. The innocent way she'd responded. The challenge she'd be if he really wanted to woo her. It was all so fresh in his head, as if it were yesterday, not almost two weeks ago.

"Come on," the guy wheedled. "One kiss."

Eva glanced up at Alex expectantly.

And his hormones sat up. Eager. Ready to pop.

"Let me get *the* picture. There's a bounty on this. Quarter of a million dollars."

He gaped at the kid. *"Quarter of a million dollars for one kiss?"*

"Yep. And it would go a long way to pay off my student loans."

Eva smiled encouragingly, as Alex's blood bubbled with enthusiasm. But that was the point. He wasn't supposed to want to kiss her. Yet he did.

Which was why he couldn't.

He turned to the photographer and said, "Sorry, bud. You're going to have to work for that shot."

His driver pointedly opened the limo door.

The photographer cursed, but Alex didn't care. He handed Eva into the car and followed her into the backseat.

But he chastised himself as he walked her to her apartment. One simple kiss would have put an end to the bounty and the speculation. And it wasn't like he would have gotten carried away. Not in public. Not in front of a member of the press.

So why hadn't he just kissed her?

She stopped at her door. "Tonight was fun."

"You're a natural at blackjack." Plus, it wasn't as if he wasn't ever going to kiss her. He had to kiss her at the engagement party, after their first dance. It was tradition. And, now that he'd made an issue of it, it could be awkward.

He should kiss her right now, a quick, chaste kiss so he'd get used to the feel of her mouth. Then at the engagement party, he could kiss her with ease, some photographer would catch it, the bounty would be lifted and that would be the end of that.

"My family has a high math aptitude."

Her answer drifted away into thin air and the hall in front of her door grew quiet.

His chest tightened. This was it. The moment. He could swoop in, give her the quick kiss that would get him accustomed to her, and swoop back out. No big deal. No problem.

But she looked up at him with her pretty blue eyes and his breath froze.

She ran her finger down his tie. "Want to come in for a minute?"

And there it was. The reason he couldn't let himself kiss her. She might be getting better at flirting, but all he saw was innocence. Sweet, wonderful innocence that she deserved to keep, to save, for the right guy.

He took a second to take in her pretty face. Her full lips. Her pert nose. Those striking eyes. He didn't exactly want to commit them to memory, but he might want to remember this, to remember that there were good people in the world who definitely deserved protecting. Even from him.

He turned and walked away, calling, "Good night," after him.

But the truth followed him down the hall to the elevator, nagging him.

He refused to acknowledge it.

So it forced its way into his brain one more time. She really was the kind of woman a man fell in love with. But he was not the kind of guy to fall in love. Love hurt, so he'd never be that vulnerable, that honest again.

And even if he tried, at some point he'd pull back, pull away, maybe even sabotage a charade she needed.

Eva watched him go, disappointment like a vise around her chest. She turned, opened her door and walked into the echoing foyer of her apartment.

So he wouldn't kiss her? It was no big deal.

Except that she wanted him to. She was getting in all kinds of flirting practice, and that was good. But this longing whooshing through her when she was around him wasn't about the practice she needed for when she actually had to find a husband. She just wanted him to kiss her.

He'd kissed every woman within kissing age in his country, and he wouldn't kiss her. It was embarrassing. Demoralizing.

It made her look at her wardrobe the next morning, toss anything that her mom might borrow and order seven really sexy blouses from a local shop, including an especially pretty one for their date that night.

But he broke their date, reminding her that this was a ruse.

"I got to thinking that maybe we've been out a little too much if photographers are so bold with us."

"We're engaged," Eva said. "We're supposed to be together all the time."

"Not really. Everybody knows this is an arranged marriage. I think we might be taking it one step too far. In fact, it might be good if the press saw me out alone."

"Alone?"

"I used to go out all the time. Now it probably looks odd that I'm always with you. This will make it look like you're not going to change me."

"That's stupid." But she felt a ring of truth to it. As if he'd said it as a message to her. Which made no sense. They hadn't even kissed for real. What would make him think she needed even more confirmation that he didn't like her?

"I think it will be very good for me to be seen at the casino, gambling with friends, but not flirting. Then the press can talk about how I only have eyes for you, instead of speculating on why I haven't kissed you in public."

Eva said, "Sounds great," but pulled in a slow breath as she disconnected the call.

Alex Sancho was the first man in her life to make her laugh and make her long to be kissed.

And he didn't want her.

He didn't have to spell it out. Didn't have to say the words. He didn't want time apart to give the press something new to speculate about. What he wanted was not to have to kiss her…or to be bored with a woman not up to his usual standards.

She set her cell phone on the dresser, sat on the edge of her bed and put her elbows on her knees and her head in her hands.

She had to get hold of herself and force herself to remember this was just a ruse, or she was going to end up getting the heartbreak she'd managed to avoid for the first twenty-five years of her life.

CHAPTER SEVEN

THE NIGHT OF the engagement party, Alex walked to her apartment to retrieve her and her mother, feeling more confident than he had since this whole business started. Now that he'd reminded himself that he wasn't the kind of guy to fall in love, and she deserved the chance to save herself for the right guy, he'd also realized he'd probably made too much of their kiss in the stable.

So it was hot? He'd had hot kisses before. He was fine. He'd very easily be able to kiss her after their first dance tonight. Not just because it was tradition. But because they'd be on the dance floor, surrounded by hundreds of guests. He could give her a nice, chaste kiss and no one would care because that was what was expected. And that would be the end of it.

Including that stupid-assed bounty.

He walked up to her apartment door. Though

she was expecting him, he remembered the last time he'd entered her apartment without knocking, and he tapped twice before he stepped inside.

When he saw Eva in another yellow gown, he had to clear his throat. Visions of her in the yellow lingerie filled his head, but he told himself she was just a woman, like every other woman. Nothing special.

"You look lovely."

"Thanks." She did a quick, flirtatious turn. "You like the gown?"

"It's—" sexy, tempting "—exquisite."

He could actually see himself loosening the laces in the back of the dress. He could see himself kissing her senseless. Taking what he wanted.

His breath stuttered in then wobbled out.

He had to stop this. He was ruined for love, a man who lived behind walls and didn't want emotions, and she'd saved herself for a prince. A real prince. His brother might not have married her, but some decent guy would. Somebody would love her beyond reason. Somebody would love her the way she deserved to be loved.

And he would act accordingly.

He escorted Eva and her mom to the assembly area outside the back door of the ballroom. Rose raced over and straightened the white flowers in Eva's hair. "Oh, my, my, sugar. You give new meaning to the word beautiful."

Karen puffed up. "My daughter is going to be the perfect bride."

Alex watched his dad's eyes soften and knew exactly what the king felt. Eva was regal, yet sweet.

King Ronaldo took her hands. "You would be a welcome addition to any family."

Alex's heart bumped against his ribs. His father knew Eva was in on their ruse. She was being protected, not getting married; and he was subtly telling her that her day would come and that some family would be lucky to get her.

Just not the Sancho family. Not Alex.

His chest tightened. His stomach hollowed out. He'd already worked his way through this. So why did hearing his dad say it make him want to punch something?

They entered the ballroom in a grand procession that became a receiving line for guests.

When her uncle—a short, thin man with a manicured beard and beady brown eyes— walked up to Alex's father, the king was gracious and polite. "Prince Gerard."

Gerard bowed. "King Ronaldo." He looked

past Rose to Eva and Alex. "And who have we here?" In an unprecedented display of disrespect, he stepped around Rose, took Eva's hand and kissed her knuckles. "You will be a beautiful bride."

Beside Alex, Eva stiffened. Alex joined her in her feelings of distaste. He'd rather be exchanging fists than pleasantries with this pasty little man, who looked like King Mason but certainly didn't have his class.

Eva bowed. "Prince Gerard."

He glanced around. "This is a spectacular place for a wedding."

"The entire kingdom is spectacular," Eva said, smiling when Alex wanted to choke the little man.

Gerard laughed. "More beautiful than Grennady?"

"Nothing is more beautiful than Grennady," she replied, still smiling. "But you should stay in Xaviera a few weeks and enjoy the sun."

"With your father gone and you getting married, there's no one else to head parliament."

Keeping her smile in place, she cocked her head. "My father isn't gone. As far as I know, he's on vacation."

"With a mistress."

"Whom he has not married because he's still

married to my mother. With no divorce, he's still king. It's my understanding he receives his daily updates the way he always has, and he's ruling as he's always ruled."

Alex swallowed a laugh.

"Well, it's assumed that with such a public display he'll be getting divorced—"

"You know the saying about what you do when you assume," Alex said, surprised his answer was so civil, but desperate to get the evil little man away from Eva.

As if reading his mind, Dom was suddenly at his side. "Luckily, your kingdom is wonderfully peaceful, and it's easy for a king to take a few weeks' vacation," Dominic said, drawing Gerard away from Eva and Alex. "I don't believe you've met my wife, Prince." He pointed at Ginny. "This is my beautiful bride, Princess Ginny."

Alex breathed a sigh of relief. Eva glanced down, straightening the full satin skirt of her gown, but he felt tension pour from her in a dark wave. Normally, he hated politics, but he'd take on the devil to protect Eva.

The receiving line lasted an hour. Standing behind the podium at the main table, Alex's father made introductions and a few comments about the engagement and wedding, and dinner was served.

The evening went well, smoothly, until it was time to dance their first dance as a couple.

Still brooding for her over the audacity of her uncle, Alex took her into his arms, and caught her gaze. Everything she'd felt as her uncle had greeted her was there in her sad blue orbs. Yet she'd kept her cool. Done her duty. Not let on that she knew Prince Gerard had put a price on her head.

She was a strong, wonderful woman. Like no one he'd ever met. And maybe that was the problem. She wasn't just another woman. She was Eva, a princess, someday a queen. But very much a woman.

He took a step, then another, then another, gliding them into the waltz he'd chosen, their eyes locked, his entire body vibrating.

She glanced around nervously. "You look like you swallowed a lemon. Please, try to at least *look* happy, even if you aren't."

He forced his lips upward, but only with great difficulty. "You should want to punch your uncle."

She laughed. "You think I don't?" She paused to smile at the crowd as he twirled her around. Then caught his gaze again. "There are times to act on feelings and times to pull back. This is a time to pull back."

"You're right."

There was so much more going on in this situation than just how he felt. He might be her protector, but she was correct. There were times to back off. To be wise.

Wasn't that what he was doing with her? Being wise. Not letting himself get involved with her personally—to protect her?

Of course he was. It was why he would give her a soft, chaste kiss at the end of their dance. He was strong enough, smart enough, to protect her from him.

The last note sounded and faded away. He raised their clasped hands, presenting her to the crowd. Then he stepped forward and delicately took her chin in his thumb and forefinger, tilting up her face and letting his mouth fall to hers.

When his lips met the softness of hers, she hesitated before lifting them to answer his kiss. The one-second pause spoke of her innocence and reminded him of every good and pure thing about her, every reason he had to want her.

But he knew he couldn't have her.

Just when he began to pull away, her lips

brushed his, eagerly as if she were starting some kind of romantic overture, but she didn't finish the kiss. She pulled away.

His breath caught at the mere thought of her trying to seduce him.

Their gazes held.

Warmth and confusion coursed through him.

Then she smiled and presented her hand to him again. He took it and bowed as she curtsied.

They left the floor amid a round of applause. Guests spilled onto the space in front of the band for dancing as Eva's mom hugged her fiercely. Then Rose hugged her. Then Ginny. Then Dom. Then the king himself embraced her.

Pulling away, he took her hand. He kissed it. "I have never seen a more beautiful first dance."

Feeling oddly left out, Alex said, "I was there too."

Rose caught him in one of her Texas-sized hugs. "Oh, sugar, you were divine, too."

But he wasn't. *She* was. *Eva* was. She was small and beautiful and cultured—a future queen.

Who turned him on like no one ever had before.

Something totally foreign rumbled through him. A need so strong, so powerful, the fight he waged to stop it went beyond anything he'd ever had to do around her.

It was ridiculous. They'd had two stupid kisses. One he instigated to prove a point. And the engagement dance tradition kiss that he'd started and she tried to finish but she'd stopped too soon.

He'd recognized days ago that he'd made too much of that first kiss, and maybe that was the problem? Maybe if they had one normal kiss, he'd see there was nothing different about her.

The small crowd of family had swallowed her up, as if protecting her, and perhaps they were. At least Alex knew Dom and his father were.

He managed to wiggle his way through the crowd and tap her shoulder. She turned, her face flushed. Her smile radiant.

"I think you and I need a minute together."

"Sure."

Preventing her from getting away from him or getting sucked into another vortex of well-wishers, he grabbed her fingers, and wove through the happy dancers with her. He walked her down one corridor, turned left and walked her down another. At the end of that hall, he opened the French doors and led her into a private garden.

Before she could say a word, he caught her by the shoulders and pressed his mouth to hers. This time there was no hesitation. No innocent pause. This time, her lips lifted to meet his.

Good. This was what they needed. A real, honest-to-God kiss that would prove to them both they were nothing special.

He deepened the kiss, nudging her mouth open with his tongue, and she responded. He pulled her closer. She slid her arms up his shoulders and looped them around his neck. Her breasts nestled against his chest. Their tongues twined—

Need exploded through him. His heart rate tripled. He ran his hands down her bare back and luxuriated in the silkiness of her skin before he realized he was in deep, dark trouble. Her kisses weren't innocent. They were greedy. And made him hungry for everything he knew she wanted to offer.

Kissing her hadn't accomplished what he'd set out to prove. He might have even made things worse.

He broke the kiss and bumped his forehead against hers. "Sorry."

"No woman wants a man to say he's sorry he kissed her, Alex."

The way she said his name caused a jolt in his stomach. Brought a fresh avalanche of desire. They'd shared so many secrets, spoken so honestly because of the ruse, that there was an intimacy between them now that made him feel he had a right to her.

"But I am sorry."

"Because you don't like me."

He pulled away, looked into her eyes. "Because I do like you. I like everything about you. Including the fact that I can be me with you. There's never been any pretense between us."

Her eyes studied his. "That's good then."

"No. It isn't. You're someday going to find the right guy. I don't want to screw that up for you." He tried to step away, but she caught his hand, stopping him.

"I know all this confuses you, but I sort of like *you*." She shook her head fiercely. "No. I don't sort of like you. I really like you. A lot. Including the fact that I can be *myself* with you."

"Don't say that."

Exasperation trembled through her voice. "*Why not?*"

"Because I'm not the kind of guy who's going to fall in love. And if you're as smart as I think you are, you know that."

To his chagrin, she laughed. "How do you know you can't fall in love?"

"If you have to ask, you don't know much about me or falling in love."

"Alex, every day I like you a little bit more. Even when you make it clear you want nothing to do with me, I have no control over this feeling that just keeps growing no matter how much I tell it to stop."

He shook his head. "And there it is. The difference between us. You're new. Innocent. The very fact that you can't stop those feelings shows how different we are. I know how to put the brakes on those feelings. Love's hurt me a time or two."

"And you don't want to get beyond your hurts?"

"It isn't a matter of *wanting* to get beyond the hurts. It's a matter of having almost twenty years after my mom's death to become cool, pragmatic. I learned a lot of tricks to make it look like I'm having fun and in the game, when really I'm not."

"But you fell in love with Nina."

"And got hurt again. All falling in love with

her did was prove to me that I didn't dare let my guard down. I don't share secrets. I don't tell anybody my dreams. Somewhere in here…" He rubbed his chest. "There's a ping that happens that warns me when I'm getting too close. And it stops me." He caught her gaze. "It's stopped me with you a million times. You've noticed some of them. Some of them have hurt you. This isn't something I'm going to grow out of or change. I'm a lot harder, a lot colder, than even my dad."

"You talk like a guy who thinks he knows everything, but maybe you don't."

"And you talk like a woman with stars in her eyes. A woman who is going to get hurt. And I won't let it be me who hurts you."

"I see."

"Look, we have another few weeks of this, then you're going to go back to Grennady, and I'm going to go back to who I was. You'll get so busy you'll forget me as much as I'll forget you. Unless we do something stupid."

Her face scrunched in confusion. "Something stupid?"

"Like get carried away. I'd say make love, but for me it would be just sex and for you it would be more. And you'd be devastated when I walk away at the end of this thing. So let's just keep things the way they should be. Light. Fun. Nothing serious so we can both get out of this with our sanity."

"Alex? Eva?"

The sound of Sally Peterson's voice echoed around the dark outdoor space. Alex stepped even farther away from Eva.

"Here you are!"

"Yes. We're here." He pushed back his shoulders and gave Sally his full prince stare. "May I ask what you're doing, following me?"

"Your father noticed you were missing. I volunteered to look for you."

Eva sneaked another peek at him. In all the confusion of wanting to kiss her for real to straighten all this out in his head, he'd forgotten there was a potential threat against her life.

No wonder his father had sent someone to look for them.

He caught Eva's hand, said, "We're fine," and headed through the garden, into the palace and down the hall toward the engagement party again, glad they'd had the honest talk.

Unless they did something stupid, they could both walk away from this. But if they followed through on these unwanted feelings that he knew were more physical than emotional, they'd both be sorry.

And part of him absolutely revolted at the thought she'd be sorry she met him. If he couldn't love her, if nothing else, he wanted to be the guy she remembered and smiled.

CHAPTER EIGHT

EVA MANAGED TO make it through the engagement party with her head high and a smile on her face. The next day, she happily accepted congratulations from her mom on the success of the event.

But when there was a quick knock on their door and Alex walked in, her stomach plummeted.

He didn't want her. Not because he didn't like her, but because he did. But the boy who'd lost his mom and a man who'd lost his first love had built walls. Even if they did fall in love, there would always be walls, a distance between them.

She saw it all the time in the way he related to her. The way he could walk away from kisses. The way he used protecting her as a convenient distraction so he didn't have to talk to her.

He walked into their living room, caught

her shoulders and put a soft kiss on her cheek. She suspected he'd done it for the benefit of her mother, but the unexpectedness of it stole her breath, made her heart ache all over again.

"Sally has informed me that gifts have begun arriving."

Her eyebrows rose, but her mother clapped her hands together with glee. "Oh, that's marvelous." She faced Eva. "This is the most fun part of getting married."

Alex laughed. "Really? Getting gifts is the best part of a wedding?"

"It's not about being materialistic." Her mom sniffed. "Gifts are kind of like a way to see what people really think of you." She tapped Alex's arm. "Trust me. You'll know who your friends are by what they get you."

Eva shook her head in shame at her mom's one true vice. She liked presents. "Sorry, Alex."

Alex shrugged. "Maybe she has a point. Maybe it will be fun."

"It'll be a blast," Karen assured him. "Are you going down now to start weeding through?"

"We could." Alex caught her gaze. "Or we could get some lunch. I'm kind of hungry."

Realizing he wanted time alone for a private

discussion, maybe even to explain his staff's plan to return the gifts since there really wasn't going to be a wedding, Eva said, "Great. I'm hungry too."

"There's a wonderful little bistro that serves the best salads."

She glanced down at her jeans and top. "Is this okay?"

He smiled. "You're with me, remember? The Prince of Scruffiness."

She laughed. "That's not exactly what I called you."

"But it's close," he said, directing her to the door.

They said goodbye to her mom, then walked in silence through the echoing corridor to the elevator.

When the door closed behind them, she said, "So what's up?"

"Up?"

"What do you need to talk about?"

He frowned. "Nothing."

"You didn't ask me to lunch to talk?"

"No. I asked you to lunch because I'm hungry."

"At the engagement party, you said—" She stopped herself. "Never mind." He might have said they were seeing too much of each other two days ago, and he might have warned her off at the engagement party, but today, the day after a real kiss and their honest conversation, he'd asked her to lunch for no reason except that he was hungry. And she was not questioning it.

He drove the Mercedes to a bistro so far out of the way she knew it wasn't a haunt for tourists but somewhere locals ate, drank and had fun together. Bodyguards escorted them to the restaurant, but instead of Alex opening the door, he pointed at a cluster of tables on the sidewalk bathed in hot sun and the breeze coming off the ocean.

She frowned. "Outside?"

"Among friends," he said, guiding her to a table in the corner. The wall of the restaurant was at their back. A clear view of the ocean was on their left. The other diners were to the right and in front of them.

"Prince Alex!" A tall man wearing a white apron scurried out to greet them.

Alex rose to shake his hand. He faced Eva. "This is Angelo. He owns the place. And this is—"

"Your beautiful bride," Angelo said before Alex could finish.

She smiled at him. "Thank you."

"Lunch is on me!" Angelo said effusively.

Alex laughed. "No. You cook. I pay." He took his seat again. "Amaze us with a salad that will fill us up, but not make us fat."

Angelo happily raced away, and Eva sucked in a long drink of the sea air.

Alex laughed. "You're getting a tad too comfortable with our weather."

"I know." She shook her head. "I'm in for so much culture shock when I get home."

Alex glanced around. "You mean when *we* get home."

She nodded, realizing she'd forgotten the charade, but ready to pick up the ball and do her part. "You know we'll live in a wing of Grennady's palace the way Dom and Ginny do."

A waiter arrived with a plate of appetizers and Alex plucked a piece of cheese and popped it into his mouth. "I suspected as much."

He ate another piece of cheese then said, "As heir, do you have duties?"

She shrugged. "Not really. About once a month I'm briefed on what's going on in the country. Four or five times a year I'm needed for photo ops."

He considered that. "That's very different from what Dom does. He's actually in on the politics. He has jobs."

"Your country's very different than ours. We don't have access to a cash cow like oil. We also aren't open to attack from enemies as you seem to be. We're rural. Our subjects mostly make their livings from farms."

"So you've said."

She stiffened. "What's wrong with that?"

"Nothing."

But she'd heard something in his voice. Something condescending. "Oh, so the playboy prince suddenly knows government?"

"I've heard about government around our dinner table since I was in diapers. I've picked up a thing or two."

"Such as?"

"Such as, it's a big booming world out there. With the internet, everybody can be educated. Your father hasn't considered that the generation coming up might want more from their lives than what their parents had?"

She took her napkin from the table, opened it and set it on her lap, busying herself so she didn't have to look at him. "Our country's claim to fame is that we are small and comfortable."

He leaned back, settling on his chair, as Angelo rushed out with two heaping plates of salad.

Alex complimented the owner, who blushed with pleasure at the praise, and they began eating.

But though the conversation had ended, Eva had a weird feeling in the pit of her stomach. A feeling that wouldn't let him get away with saying part of something and not finishing it.

Finally she said, "So what would you do?"

With a forkful of salad halfway to his mouth, Alex said, "Do?"

"About the next generation in my country?"

He drew in a breath, thought for a second, then said, "If I were in charge of a country like yours, a place that's quiet and peaceful, I'd probably try to lure an internet company into making its home there. You could provide hundreds if not thousands of jobs when you consider that ancillary businesses would shoot up. Not to mention extra jobs from the restaurants, shops and auto mechanics needed to support the population that would migrate to wherever the company settled."

"Most corporations want a warmer climate."

"Internet companies don't necessarily want a warmer climate. They want ambiance. Your country has it in abundance. Skiing. Snowmobiles. Snowboarding. Sleigh riding. And in the summer, hiking and horseback riding. Rock climbing. Your country has enough ways to commune with nature, which internet companies believe inspires creativity, to entice just about anybody you want."

She drew in a breath. "Impressive."

He laughed. "Impressive that I can't help overhearing conversations at dinner?"

"You make light, Alexandros Sancho, but you're not the player you try to make everyone believe."

He smiled. "There are already plenty of rulers in my family. We don't need another."

But the next day after a meeting with the royal guard, Dom asked Alex to come to parliament, and he went. Not because he someday wanted to be a ruler. But because he enjoyed the feeling of being productive.

His mornings soon filled with meetings over Eva's protection because designers and florists and all sorts of wedding prep people began trooping to her apartment almost nonstop for consultations.

Every day he'd take her to lunch, then he'd return to find Dom and walk with him to parliament, to the section of their government that connected them to their people.

And the whole time he wondered about

Eva's country, about Grennady. How could her father let them get so far behind the times?

He wouldn't let himself think about it while eating dinner with her. He was a prince supposedly marrying a beautiful princess. It wouldn't do to have anyone overhear them talk about politics.

But one day, when he walked in on a conference call his father was having with King Mason and Dom, it all poured into his head again. He didn't argue when his dad motioned for him to sit in.

He also sat in the next day and the next. He didn't say much. He didn't think it was his place to give advice, though it was clear King Mason needed it. He offered the idea of enticing an internet company to Grennady, then he sat and listened without comment for the next two days' calls, until the fate of his "wedding" to Eva came up for discussion.

When the phone in the apartment buzzed, Eva jumped. So did her mom. The phone never rang, except to announce a wedding vendor, and they had no one scheduled for that day. Eva looked at her mom. Her mom looked back.

"I'm guessing we should answer it."

Eva carefully made her way to the discreet

beige phone that sat inconspicuously on a table by the sofa.

"Hello?"

"Good afternoon, Princess. This is Maria Gable, King Ronaldo's personal assistant. He requests your presence in his office. A member of his guard should be arriving for you shortly."

"Oh." Confusion rumbled through her, but one didn't say no to a king, not when she was at his palace, and not when he was protecting her. Especially since he could have news about her dad.

Three weeks had passed since her father had stashed her and her mom in Xaviera. Her father had had plenty of time to get the proof that his brother had conspired to have him killed. Plenty of time to arrest Prince Gerard. The day she'd been simultaneously praying for and dreading might be here.

"Thank you."

She hung up the phone, glancing at her blue jeans and white tank top. She and Alex had decided to spend the afternoon poking around the shops in the village. Very visible again. They'd hold hands. They'd smile, and they'd talk.

Her nerves jumped at the thought of it. She loved talking to him. She loved that he saw things, knew things, that she didn't. And even though he might have all kinds of strategies in place to resist her, she wasn't so experienced, so lucky. Every day she liked him a little more.

But it might all be over. She might have been summoned to the king's office because her dad was back. Safe. Maybe even already in Grennady.

An odd queasiness filled her.

After today, she might never again see Alex.

A knock at the door announced the royal guard member who led her to the king's office. She hadn't been in the administrative offices of the palace, but she was so nervous that the art on the walls barely caught her attention.

She walked into a sitting room, then a huge space full of secretaries and assistants, then an office with one woman, who rose.

In her forties, with reddish-blond hair and brown eyes, she bowed. "Princess." She walked to the door of the office behind hers, and the guard with Eva stepped back, as if handing her off. "I'm Maria."

"A pleasure to meet you."

"You too, Princess." She opened the door. "This way."

They walked through another room to a gilded door in the back, which Maria opened.

Eva walked into an office so grand, she blinked. The king, Dominic and Alex all rose from the seats around a huge mahogany desk.

Alex walked over and took her hands. Catching her gaze, he said, "Your father is on the phone."

Her heart lurched. "He is?"

"Yes."

Her dad being back in Grennady was good news, but Alex's expression was serious, concerned, as if he was afraid she might shatter into a million pieces.

Confusion pummeled her as King Ronaldo rounded his desk. "You take my seat and we'll give you some privacy. Just press the blinking button on the phone. That's the line he's on."

Eva's stomach fell. Something was dreadfully wrong.

Nonetheless, she held her head high. "Thank you."

As she walked behind the desk, the Sancho men left the office.

She sat. Took a breath. Pushed the blinking light on the phone.

"Dad?"

"Hey, sweetie. How are the cats?"

Her eyes filled with tears. "I haven't seen my cats in weeks." She gulped a breath, so scared and so confused she didn't know what to say, what to ask. A million possibilities loomed in her mind. None of them good.

"How are you? *Where* are you?"

"I'm fine. But I'm still in hiding. Investigating everything that's going on, I realized that my brother being a traitor is only part of the problem. But I don't want to clean house in parliament, or reorganize the government. I want to show my detractors that I'm willing to work with them. There's been dissension growing for years. I've seen it, of course, but I didn't realize it had hit a crisis point."

"What kind of dissension?"

"Our country is horribly behind the times."

Hadn't Alex told her that? "And we have a generation coming up that wants something more."

He laughed. "When did you get so smart?"

"I'm not. Alex mentioned it. He suggested luring an internet company to Grennady, convincing them to put their corporate headquarters there."

Her dad laughed again. "He suggested it to me too. I'm in negotiations with a company right now. But I can't go back until I have a solid plan, proof that when I return things will be different."

Her entire body froze. "Oh."

"But the danger has passed, sweetie."

"It has?" She sat back in the chair. She should have been relieved, but the feeling that Alex had been in on all of this sent little lightning bolts of anger through her. She was to be the queen of her country someday, yet everyone knew this plan but her. "Really?"

"Yes, your uncle is under secret house arrest, until I come home. But I still need time to create a new vision for the country."

She sat up. "How can I help?"

"By doing what you're doing. I don't want word of this to get out. I don't want to give my dissenters a chance to find a voice before I can come home strong, with a plan. That's why I'm calling. You and Alex are going to have to go through with the wedding."

She took a few seconds to let that sink in. Three weeks ago she could have married him in an award-winning performance. Now? He'd protected her. Kissed her. Told her he didn't want her. And gone behind her back to help her dad, when she should have been the one in on the discussions.

Her dad drew in a breath. "Sweetie, I had no idea things were so bad. We're a small, quiet country. I thought we could go on the way we were, the way we have been for generations. But there's dissension that runs deep enough that my own brother wanted to kill me." He took another breath. "I should have known how bad it had gotten. But I didn't. And now I have to fix it."

"Wouldn't it be better for you to go home now?"

"I can't go home until I have a solid plan. If I go home, admitting that we have things to fix, but without a way to fix them, the rebels will see we're shaky and take advantage."

She got what he was saying. He just seemed to be taking the long way around. Still, a princess didn't question her king.

"We've always been so small that we haven't really had a plan. We simply solved problems as they arose. Now, we know we need to think of all of the needs of the people and meet them. Ronaldo has sent financial advisors. Prince Dominic is flying here to help us tomorrow. We have the information. We just have to sort through it and figure out what works for us."

And now he'd called *Dominic* for help. Not just Alex but Dominic? Her nerve endings fluffed out like porcupine quills. But she said, "Okay."

"I'm sorry I won't be at the wedding."

"It's not a real wedding." But that thought depressed her even more. She'd be standing up in front of a mountain of press, her friends, her family, Alex's family, saying vows that weren't real. To a guy she was growing to like, but who didn't like or trust her enough to tell her he'd been helping her dad for God only knew how long.

"What happens if you can't do this? Three weeks have gone by. How do you know your detractors aren't already planning to take over?"

"Oh, I'm pretty sure they are. That's why this wedding is so important. You're distracting everybody. Buying time. And I swear, I won't need more than another few weeks."

A few weeks of being married to Alex? She squeezed her eyes shut. If he were a mean, ugly man, none of this would matter. She could do this with her eyes closed. But he was good-looking, kind, smart. A born leader who, quite obviously, her father trusted.

And maybe the real reason he didn't want her was bigger than she'd suspected. Maybe he saw her as her dad did. A figurehead? Not a real person, not someone who could give or take love. Someone who simply held a place and did what she was told.

She swallowed hard, but said what her dad needed to hear. "I'm fine. I serve at the pleasure of my king."

"That's my girl. And when everything's straightened out, I'll come to America and visit your cats."

Pain skittered through her. The very thing she'd done to keep herself busy, to make a mark while she bided time, made her look foolish.

She swallowed again, played her role with a dad who was too busy to see how he was hurting her. "So you've said a million times."

"This time I mean it. We'll attach the trip to a formal, official visit to the United States."

She took a slow, necessary breath, as the truth of her life made a ring of sadness around her heart. She was nothing. "Okay."

"Great. I'll talk to your mom this afternoon."

"I think she's going to skin you alive."

"No. She'll understand."

Eva hung up the phone a few minutes later knowing that her mom *would* understand. Her mom would do her duty. So would Eva.

But her hands shook and her heart hurt. In four weeks, her entire life had changed. She'd believed it was because her dad had gone through a midlife crisis, but it was so much more serious than that. And the Sancho family had stepped in to help them. But she'd been tucked away like a porcelain doll.

A few seconds after she'd hung up the phone, Alex and his father returned to his office.

Alex said, "Are you okay?"

She nodded. "He says he's going to talk to my mom this afternoon."

The king reached for his phone. "I'll tell my secretary to arrange that. You two do whatever it is you had planned for today."

She nodded again and Alex took her elbow to guide her out of the office.

In the corridor leading away from the administrative offices, Alex glanced at her jeans and tank top and said, "So I see you're ready to go into the village."

She forced a smile. "Sure."

He stopped. "You're not ready?"

She shook her head as the implications of everything her dad had said rained down on her. What did she expect? Her father had no intention of retiring. She was a well-loved only child…only *daughter*. She busied herself with charities, but essentially lived in America. Even *she* didn't see herself as a ruler.

"No. No. I'm fine."

He studied her face. "You're not fine."

"Does it matter? There are so much bigger things at stake here."

"True, but you're not going to convince a block of reporters that you're a happy bride if your smile falters."

"I can pull it off."

He glanced down the empty corridor. "You know what? Maybe you can, but this has been a long, weird bunch of weeks for you. You're accustomed to low-key. I've dragged you around town. Maybe today would be a good day to take a break."

She hated to say it. Hated to think she was this weak. Except she wasn't weak. She was worn down by the truth. Her father didn't trust her. She'd thought he did because he let her live her own life, but if he really trusted her, she'd be preparing to be queen. To be a ruler. But she wasn't. Her dad had said she'd rule only long enough until her son—a son who wasn't even yet born—could take over.

"No. I need to go somewhere. I can't sit around the palace all day. That would just make things worse."

He smiled. "I think I have an idea." He glanced at her outfit again and confusing longings rolled through her. This man pampered her, protected her, and kept her out of the loop even more than her father did. Why should she want him to look at her with interest in his eyes?

"You'll do."

Thank God that made her laugh. "I'll do?"

He took her hand. "Yes. I have an idea."

He rushed her out of the corridor to a slim hall that led to another slim hall.

"What are we doing?"

"Escaping."

Shades of the real Alex returned, the simple guy she really liked. Not the one who apparently went to secret meetings with her dad. "Escaping?"

"Yes. There are times when I can't stand the bodyguards, hate the media…don't even want my dad to know where I am."

Her eyebrows rose. This truly was the Alex she liked.

"So—" He opened a small, inconspicuous door onto a huge garage. "I go here."

She glanced around in awe at the sheer number of vehicles. Everything from limos to tiny sports cars and bikes. "To a garage?"

"Nope," he said, grabbing a motorcycle helmet from a shelf.

Realizing what was happening, she skittered back. "Oh, no…"

He plopped the helmet on her head. "You don't ride?"

"No."

"Then this is the perfect day for you to start." He put a helmet on his head. When he spoke his voice came to her through a speaker by her ear. "You'll love this."

She had the horrible feeling of going from the frying pan into the fire, but if anything would make her forget that her dad didn't need her help—didn't want her help—fear for her life would probably accomplish it.

He climbed on a small, rather simple bike.

She looked at him. "*This* is the royal motorcycle?"

"This is a bike no one looks at twice. In jeans and a T-shirt, with a helmet on my head, I'm just another guy out for a ride on a bike."

She climbed on behind him. "Good point."

He was right. Maybe what she needed was even for *her* to forget she was a princess.

CHAPTER NINE

ALEX REVVED THE engine and headed for a garage door that automatically opened when they got close. A warm sun beat down on them, but as soon as he turned them onto the road that wove through the trees, the air cooled.

Eva clung to him, obviously a first-time rider. But the farther they got into the woods, the more her grip loosened.

He missed it. As happy as he was that she'd relaxed, he missed having her arms wrapped tightly around him for support. He knew something was wrong. He'd expected her to be thrilled her dad was safe, and had a plan in process. Instead, she seemed confused, disoriented. So he vowed that no matter what it took today, he would distract her.

They drove and drove. Up a mountain, through another patch of trees. The feeling of the wind swirling around him always calmed him, and he could feel her relaxing behind him.

Finally, the house came into view. A nine-bedroom, two-story stone monstrosity with brown shutters and a wide wooden porch that ran across the entire front and curved around the right side, the house had been designed as a retreat, a place for the Sancho family to be a family. Not royalty. Not rulers. Just people.

He heard her small gasp through the system of mics in their helmets.

"It's gorgeous."

"It's old," he said flatly. "And in general need of repairs."

He drove the bike down the winding road that took them to the aging country house. He punched the alarm code into the box by the gate. It swung open, and they rode through, then the gate automatically closed behind them.

Standing on the front porch, he used another code for the house alarm.

As he reached for the knob to open the door, she glanced around nervously. "You're not worried about security?"

"We're fine here. I'll bet nobody even realizes we're gone. I told my guards we'd ring when we were ready to head for town. If I don't ring, they'll just think we decided not to go out."

He opened the door revealing a dusty foyer.

Furniture was covered with cloths. Cobwebs danced like streamers from the chandelier to all four corners.

He batted them away so Eva wouldn't have to walk through them. "Just FYI, the press knows this is the house we would be living in if we got married."

"Really?"

"Yes. It's already crowded in the palace. It's a gift to be given a real home."

She stepped around a chair that had been placed haphazardly in the foyer, as if someone had been moving it to storage and forgotten it.

"How long has it been since anyone's been here?"

He didn't even have to think about it. "Since my mom's death."

She faced him. Her eyes filled with apology, the first real emotion he'd seen from her since her call with her dad. "Sorry."

"Don't be. Some things are just facts."

Her eyes softened. "Facts to me. Sorrow for you."

He sniffed a laugh. "At one time. But I'm accustomed to it, remember? I'm the guy with the walls." He led her out of the foyer to the huge room beside it. The dusty fireplace was the only thing not covered by cloths.

"You have a fireplace!"

"We only used it to hang stockings at Christmas."

She walked over, ran her hand along the rich wood of the mantel, sending dust flying. "So you had Christmases here?"

"Actually we came here a lot. My mother believed that living where he worked kept my dad from relaxing. So most weekends she'd bring him here."

But Christmas memories were the strongest and they floated to him. Trays of cookies and tea. Mountains of presents wrapped in shiny foil. His mother laughing.

They walked through a sitting room and formal dining room, an office, and a craft room that had been his mother's, down a long corridor to a ballroom.

"You have a ballroom in a country house?"

"My father always hosted a grand party."

She walked inside. Her voice echoed around her when she said, "Wow."

But he suddenly pictured the room clean, decorated for the holidays as it had been when his mom was alive. He could see Eva in her red gown, greeting guests at the door because parties here had been formal, but comfortable… wonderful.

He shook his head to clear the haze. "Let me show you the kitchen."

Rather than a huge restaurant kitchen designed for a staff, the room was small, intimate. His mother had created it that way. After the big party, she would dismiss the servants—let them have their holiday. Then she would make Christmas or Easter breakfast and dinner. He and Dom would stay in their PJs and lean against the center island as she cooked.

"Oh, I could see myself making pizza on that island."

"You make pizza?"

She laughed. "I love to cook."

"My mom did too."

"Let me guess. That was part of your holiday tradition. That she cooked."

He walked around the room slowly, memories tripping over themselves in his head. He might have only been eight when his mom died, but he remembered enough to fill a lifetime.

"When we were here we were normal."

"You're not now?"

He caught her gaze. "My father's a king. My brother will be a king. And I'm the extra guy who hangs around in case my brother dies." He shook his head. "We're kind of creepy."

"It's only creepy if you focus on it."

"Which is why I lived the kind of life I did before this mess with your dad started. I didn't want to think about it, let alone focus on it."

"You still fit. If you've felt left out before this, it was by your own choosing."

"Says the woman who went to America to be herself and have a good time before she becomes a queen."

She stiffened. "Is that how you see me?"

He shrugged. "It appears, Princess, to be how you want to be seen. You're the woman who doesn't want to be queen, remember? You just want to rule long enough for your oldest son to be groomed for the top spot."

She stiffened again. And he had absolutely no idea why. She'd told him that herself.

But rather than admit it or tell him to shut up, she looked around the kitchen. "I know how I'd remodel this room."

He laughed at her quick change of subject. "Really?"

"White cabinets. Probably a marble countertop. Updated appliances. And a long oak table over there." She pointed at a space by French doors that looked out over a garden. "With four chairs and a bench for kids, so they could nudge each other and misbehave."

He laughed. "You can tell you haven't been around kids much. Misbehaving children aren't fun."

"For adults. But I'll bet it's fun to be one."

He remembered himself and Dom wrestling like two bear cubs and couldn't lie. "It is."

And suddenly he saw the room the way she saw it. White cabinets. Marble countertops. Chairs filled with kids. Laughter mixing with the scent of burning toast.

"You want a family, don't you?"

She glanced around again at the cobweb-filled room, smiling, obviously not seeing the dust. "Being an only child is miserable." She motioned around the kitchen. "For decades I thought this was what I wanted. A real house. A place for memories and kids. Lot of kids. Breakfast, lunch, dinner." She sighed. "Birthday parties and horseback riding lessons. Managing schedules and dance classes."

"You wanted to be a mom."

She squeezed her eyes shut, as if furious. "I'm a queen."

He frowned, confused. "But not forever. You said you only want to rule in the space between your dad and your future son."

Her gaze met his. "You knew my dad intended to coax an internet company to Grennady."

Another change of subject. Still, he kept up. "I gave him the idea."

Her face whitened. "In secret meetings with him?"

"Not meetings. Conference calls. One every day for the past few days."

When her mouth fell open in what looked to be disbelief, he defensively said, "I am in charge of your protection."

She whirled away from him. "I'm the next ruler of my country! I should have been in on those calls!"

And suddenly it all made sense to Alex. Not only was she out of the loop, but also their positions had reversed. When they met, he was a happy-go-lucky prince with no ambition and she was a princess devoted to duty. Now, he had jobs and her dad had hidden her away.

"Hey, look, I'm sorry." He raised his hands in apology. "If it's any consolation, I liked you enough to want to protect you."

She sniffed a laugh. "Yeah. Sure. That makes it all better."

"And my dad's not the only one thrilled that I've gotten off my duff and found a place in our kingdom. Dom is also thrilled. I am thrilled. And we owe it all to you. You motivated me to do things I would have never believed possible."

He watched the truth of that settle in on her, and pushed when another man might have let her wallow in her deserved misery. "You redeemed me. You probably had the biggest role of all of us."

"Yeah. It's pretty great."

He laughed. "Don't try to kid a kidder. It's no fun being the one in the background. I've lived that life. But though you're in the background, you still played a part. Everything you've done has served a purpose. Plus, your dad brought you into the big picture situation during that telephone conversation this afternoon. And he still needs time, which you are buying by going through with a wedding to me."

She sort of laughed, so he walked over, put a finger under her chin and lifted her face until their eyes met.

"So what? You don't want to marry me now?"

Eva's heart skipped a beat. He seemed to realize how different he was, how strong. Not that he hadn't been attractive before. But this smart, committed version of the sexy guy she'd been seeing was nearly irresistible.

"I'll do whatever my king needs me to do."

"I also think it's time you and your dad had a chat about your job."

She laughed. "Two weeks as a working member of your palace staff and suddenly you think everybody needs a job?"

"I don't think everybody needs a job. I think your years in America were the whim of a young princess finding her feet. I think this crisis showed you who you want to be."

Oh, lord. He was right. And she didn't have a clue what to do about it. "It has."

"So now you have to make sure the talk you have with your dad sinks in. Make sure he understands you're not a pampered daughter holding a place until a new man comes along to take over. You're a smart woman, more than capable of ruling."

And when he talked like that, she wanted to melt at his feet.

He grinned at her. "Need help talking to your dad?"

She laughed again, but this time she also swatted him. "Stop."

"What? I can be very helpful."

She knew he meant it jokingly but the truth

was this Alex, this smart Alex, could be very helpful. She could see him heading up her palace's royal guard. See him being a trusted husband, advisor.

And she found herself at the place where the charade became scary. These weeks had grown him enough, changed him enough that he would be the perfect husband for her.

Now she had nothing to battle with. Nothing to help her resist the feelings she was getting for him. Three weeks ago he might have been the absolute worst choice for a queen to take as a mate. Right now? He was perfect.

Not to mention gorgeous. Sexy. Fun. He'd known she'd needed time away and he'd given it to her.

How was she supposed to resist this guy?

"Come on," he said. "What would you cook if you were mum here?"

She shook her head, hoping to shake off her ridiculously sober mood. They'd use this time to make a plan about talking to her dad, about her place in her kingdom, which she would implement when they returned to Grennady. But he didn't want to be her husband and she had to respect that. She needed to show him she was fine.

She walked to the big center island, pictured it white with a big marble countertop. "I'd make pancakes."

"I love pancakes."

"How about apple?"

"I could be persuaded to try one."

She laughed, but her heart shattered. She could see them in this kitchen. Before she became queen there'd be plenty of time to be a real family, to teach their kids the things she and Alex hadn't learned because their parents didn't know to teach them. She could see the dark-eyed, dark-haired little boy who would take the throne after her. She could see the dark-haired, blue-eyed little girl who'd be Daddy's favorite. She could see Alex as a daddy, know he'd love the role.

But he couldn't see it. Because he didn't want it.

It was one thing to grow enough that he could take his place in his country's royal family. Quite another to take down those walls around his heart.

CHAPTER TEN

ALEX EXPECTED HIMSELF to be nervous the day of his fake wedding. What he hadn't expected was the weirdness that accompanied it. When the royal photographers snapped pictures of him, his father and Dom, he decided he got an odd shiver because it was all so real. Everything might be fake, but it needed to appear real, so they'd spared no expense. Left no tradition unturned. Including the exchange of personal gifts. Because it all had to be documented to look real.

His father went first. Handing him the keys to the country house, which were largely symbolic since the retreat now had key pads, he said, "This house gave your mother and me great pleasure." The photographers snapped nonstop. "It's my hope it will give you and Eva many years of happiness too."

Flash. Flash. Flash.

He took the keys, hugged his dad, and suddenly felt something he'd never felt before. Overwhelming respect for the king, followed by blind sorrow for the man who'd lost his wife and been forced to raise two sons alone. He squeezed his eyes shut, wrapped his arms around his dad more tightly.

It was the first real hug he'd given his dad since his mom passed.

When his dad pulled back, his eyes were filled with tears. Rose stepped forward. Wearing a very simple pale blue gown, she looked elegant and regal. She handed his dad a handkerchief. "Here, sweetie."

The king took it and waved off the photographers. "Don't get pictures of that. No one wants to see me maudlin."

"Then you're not going to want to watch him open this," Dom said, taking the small rectangular box from Ginny, who had her lips pressed together as if forcing herself not to cry. Eva's maid of honor, she wore a pale green dress with her hair pulled off her face and cascading down her back, a vision of yellow curls.

Dom handed the box to Alex. He removed the lid and there was an eight-by-ten picture of their family, a candid shot at one of their Christmas parties. Their mother beaming.

Dom trying to look kingly. And Alex sticking out his tongue.

The room grew silent.

It seemed the photographers held their collective breaths.

"It's—"

"It's so very you," Ginny said with a sniff that was half laugh, half sob. "Sticking out your tongue. Being a pain in the butt."

Emotion tightened his chest. He remembered the day as one of the happiest of his life. But when he pictured the ballroom in the house, he didn't see himself, his mom or even guests. He saw Eva standing in the cobwebs.

He hugged Dom, then Ginny, thanking them.

His father's manservant, Henry, who'd been at the palace for as long as Alex could remember, took the gifts with the promise that they would be in Alex's apartment when he returned from his honeymoon.

Alex nodded. The photographers left. The little family dispersed. His father needed to be in the church's front row with Rose when Alex and Dom walked onto the altar, but first they had to retrieve Jimmy from the nanny because Ginny was maid of honor but Rose wanted the baby at the wedding.

When the bells chimed out four o'clock, Dom and Alex walked onto the altar. Rose and the king were in their seats, Rose holding Jimmy who patted her cheeks. The organist began a processional and Eva's two university friends walked in followed by Ginny.

Then the music changed and Eva was at the door of the church. With no father to walk her down the aisle, she'd decided to walk in unescorted.

At the time it had seemed like the bad choice, but after their discussion at the country house, when he'd seen just how strong and smart she was, it no longer seemed wrong.

In her long white dress, with her black hair pulled into a tight knot with a ring of pearls around the knot, connected to a veil that fell from the pearls to the long, long train of her dress, Eva was the epitome of quiet elegance. Perfection. Strength.

Yet somehow she managed to look innocent and beautiful.

His breath fluttered in and stuttered out. Longings filled him.

She walked up to him. The minister said, "Who gives this woman in matrimony?"

She held Alex's gaze. "I give myself."

Emotion trembled through him. Because

he finally saw. For as much as he'd believed he didn't have a place in his family, she'd felt worse. She had no siblings. And all her country seemed to want her to do was produce the next heir.

But she was a queen.

He took her hand, kissed her knuckles. Then turned her to face the altar.

After a long ceremony and hours of pictures, they wound their way down the palace halls and corridors to the back door of the ballroom for a receiving line and reception.

This time there was no Uncle Gerard. Alex was sure his absence would be reported in the papers tomorrow, and wondered how the world would react when King Mason finally announced his brother hadn't attended Eva's wedding because he was under house arrest for treason.

What a world his wife would be returning to.

When it came time for their first dance as a couple, he led her to the dance floor. When their gazes met, he saw her fatigue.

As he swung her around to the tune of the waltz, he said, "It's been a long day."

She forced a smile. "Yes, it has."

"Where's the woman who wanted to make apple pancakes?"

She laughed. "I think I left her back at the country house."

"Maybe we should go get her?"

She laughed again.

His spirits lifted. He twirled her around. "It is a little nerve-racking to be guest of honor in front of eight hundred people."

She met his gaze again. "And sitting for hours for a bunch of pictures no one will see."

He danced her in a big looping circle around the floor, twirled her out, then pulled her back in, making her giggle.

"Stop! That's not a waltz."

"And we care because?"

She giggled again. "I don't know. Honestly. I just don't know anything anymore."

"Sure you do. You have tons of stuff you have to face when you go back home. But that could be days away. Weeks away." He dipped his head to catch her gaze again. "Why don't we have some fun?"

Why not?

She could think of a million reasons, but most of them revolved around keeping her heart when she desperately wanted to lose it to him.

Still, when he twirled her around again, she laughed. When the dance ended and he gave an exaggerated bow, she laughed again. The wedding guests loved him.

She loved him.

And there it was. The truth that stood on the edge of her mind every day, but which she wouldn't let manifest because it was too frightening. How could she love a man who didn't love her?

When the dance was over, her mother met her on the edge of the dance circle and led her to the private table set up for Alex and Eva. She handed her a glass of water.

"Drink this."

Eva shook her head. "I'm not thirsty."

"You need to stay hydrated," her mom insisted.

Alex took the glass from her. He cast a funny glance at Eva's mom. "We'll both take regular breaks and have *sips* of water. Not glasses or gulps."

Karen sighed, but Eva nodded, as the photographer came over to take a candid shot of them in a down minute. She smiled, but inside her heart broke a little. There would be thousands of pictures of a fake wedding.

Alex pulled her out to the dance floor again. "What are you doing?"

He drew her into his arms. "You think too

much. And tonight we're not thinking. We're dancing."

She recognized his point immediately. Her face probably showed her unhappiness. He didn't know it was over the fact that she loved him. He thought she was upset about documenting an event that was essentially fake. But that was good. It gave her breathing room. And maybe even a chance to let herself feel the love she couldn't deny—if only for a minute or two.

He tightened his arms around her, and she realized the music had shifted and they were dancing a slow song.

Even considering all the times they'd kissed, she hadn't ever had the presence of mind to appreciate being close to him. The first time he'd kissed her to persuade her not to marry him, he'd yanked her against him. They'd been pressed together from chest to knees and she'd felt the strength and power in his tense body.

Then he'd sneaked the kiss at the engagement party. The real kiss. And the press of their bodies had nothing to do with strength or power. That had been a kiss of real emotion. And she'd felt it in every place their bodies brushed.

But now they were dancing. Her brain was clear enough to take in the breadth of his shoulders, the solidness of his chest, the leanness of his torso. She let the hand she had at his shoulder drift down and come up again.

His head tilted as he caught her gaze.

What would he do if he knew she was nearly overwhelmed by love for him?

What would he do if he knew curiosity about how he felt beneath all these clothes raced through her?

What would he think if she told him she was tired of being a woman one step behind everybody else her own age because she'd been sheltered, protected by an arranged marriage?

What if she told him she wanted to make love with him once, just once, for the pleasure of being with the first man she truly loved? So that she could move into the rest of her life a whole person, a real woman, the woman she was meant to be?

If she promised him no emotion, no attempt to break down his walls, and asked for just one night of everything...

Would he be able to say no?

CHAPTER ELEVEN

THEY WERE SCHEDULED to spend the night at the palace and leave for their honeymoon the day after the wedding, but for security purposes Alex had changed that, deciding they should leave immediately after the wedding.

The royal guard whisked them to the family helicopter which took them to the yacht. Alex led Eva to the king's suite of rooms, and at the door, lifted her into his arms.

She laughed. "Isn't carrying me over the threshold an American custom?"

He shrugged, deftly turned the doorknob with one hand and used his foot to nudge the door open. "Who cares?" He said it light and breezily, knowing he didn't have to remind her he was doing it for the staff, but feeling the odd sense of longing that had followed him around all day.

She laughed again, and the sound reverberated through him. It reminded him of sunny days and happiness, so he put her down quickly, in front of the sofa of the sitting room.

She turned to him with a smile, but he walked to the bar. She knew the drill as well as he did. Theirs was a fake marriage. The dancing and flirting they'd done at the wedding had been wrong. Dangerous to her future and his sanity. Now that there were no crowds to please or fool, he had to step away from her.

A bottle of his father's best champagne lay in a bucket of ice on the bar. He sniffed a laugh. His father certainly knew how to carry a charade to its full conclusion.

He lifted the bottle. "Champagne?"

Her satin gown swished and swirled as she made her way to the bar. "Yes. Thank you."

He popped the cork, found two glasses and poured.

He handed her a glass and she saluted him. "To us?"

"Sure, why not?" He said it swiftly, easily, but seeing her so casually sitting on one of the seats of his royal family's yacht, looking like she belonged there, sent a ping of that yearning through him again.

He ignored it.

"There are two bedrooms in this suite."

She raised her eyes, caught his gaze. "I figured."

Her eyes were filled with the emotion that always stopped his heart. Hopeful, yet somehow resigned. She was a woman so married to duty that she rarely got what she wanted, but a part of her still hungered for it.

She took a sip of her champagne, then another, her full lips barely touching the flute. The delicateness of her face was at odds with the strength of her character, which somehow managed to mask a very feminine, very sexy woman. And right at that moment he'd give anything to run his hands down her arms, along her torso, while he kissed her, if only to show her that she was worthy—worth it. That she was beautiful and powerful and perfect.

He took a step back. Dom had said there had been a moment on his wedding night when he'd looked at Ginny and simply hadn't been able to resist her. At the time, Alex had thought his brother a besotted fool, or a man who simply hadn't been with enough women. But tonight, looking at Eva, knowing her the way he did, he wondered how much willpower he'd have to muster to walk away from what he so desperately wanted.

She finished her champagne and slid off

the stool, her gown a glorious complement of silks and satins that rustled around her. She pointed to the right. "I imagine my bedroom is that way."

"Yes."

"I'm pretty good at this guessing stuff."

"You had a fifty-fifty chance of being right."

She smiled. "Better odds than blackjack."

"Much better odds."

She waited just the tiniest bit, while he waged a battle in his head. Not because he wanted her so much...though he did. But because she wanted him. It was there in her eyes. And it was easier to deny his own need than hers. The moment was fraught with possibilities. Glorious, wonderful things.

With slow, deliberate movements she walked over to him. He took a breath, held it.

But she didn't rise to her tiptoes to press her lips to his. Didn't touch him. Instead, she pulled the long, looping net veil to the side as she presented her back to him.

"Can you undo this for me?"

He swallowed. His fingers went to the small hook-and-eye closure above the long zipper of her strapless gown. "You know the night we left your dress in my hallway?"

She hesitated. "Yes."

"I told myself I could have had that little yellow gown off you in about twenty seconds."

The hook and eye disengaged. She turned and met his gaze. "Sure of yourself?"

"Experienced."

Their eyes held. If there was one strike that counted against him with her, it was his experience. He'd slept with everyone from starlets to vacationing waifs. She'd given herself to no one.

"Sometimes experience is a good thing."

"You didn't think so when you first met me."

"I was wrong."

He held her gaze. "No. You weren't."

She turned, presenting her back to him again so he could get the zipper. "I've been wrong about a lot of things, remember? I thought I didn't want to be a queen. Thought I'd be content being a placeholder. Turns out I'm not."

He glanced down at the zipper for her gown. Once he began pulling it down, he'd be seeing her back, the slope of her torso that led to her perfect bottom.

He stalled. "And you've got something of a fight ahead of you when you go home."

"I'm ready."

He wasn't. He thought no woman could tempt him beyond his power to resist. But as his fingers itched to pull down the zipper of her dress, his libido sat on the bleachers of his brain, munching popcorn, waiting for the show to begin.

His brain screamed that he should turn her around, send her to her room and dispatch a maid to help her with her dress.

His libido groaned, told him that was a damned fool idea. He'd seen her back before. One more peek wouldn't hurt.

He took the zipper in his tingling fingers.

She looked over her shoulder at him. "Do you want me to call a maid?"

Yes. "No." This was stupid. He had seen her back before and for the love of all that was holy, it was only a back.

He pulled the zipper down past her strapless bra and when he saw the yellow lace, he laughed. "Yellow undies for your wedding?"

"With all the white that was floating around, I wanted a little bit of color. I love yellow."

He was beginning to love yellow too.

He pulled the zipper to her waist, thinking that would be the end of it, but to his surprise it ran the whole way to her bottom. The whole way to yellow satin panties, trimmed in lace, looking so sexily feminine, his gut tensed.

The room suddenly got hot.

The top of her strapless dress collapsed into her hands and she brought her arms up to catch it. When she turned to face him, the bodice was a crumbled heap against the pretty yellow bra and bare shoulders that were creamy white as if they'd never seen the sun.

The temptation that had been hovering on the edge of everything they'd done the past four weeks overwhelmed him. All he wanted was a simple touch.

He put his hands on her shoulders, onto skin that felt like new velvet.

And maybe a taste.

He leaned down, his gaze trapped with her expectant one, and knew this was absolutely wrong, but telling himself he could handle it.

When his lips met hers, she lifted her arms to his shoulders and the dress fell, puddling on the floor between them. The lace of her bra crushed against the silk of his shirt but he swore he didn't feel the barrier between them. He felt that lace brushing his chest—

He pulled back, sucked in a breath of air. As much as he wanted this, he couldn't have her.

Bending down, he picked up her gown, pressing it against her chest until she took it.

"This is wrong."

She leaped to her tiptoes and brushed her lips across his. "No, it's not."

"I think you're forgetting something very important. You told me you wanted to become queen."

She held his gaze, waiting for his explanation.

"I want you to fulfill your destiny."

"And you don't want to be a husband to a queen? Don't worry. I don't expect you to stay married to me. I just want this. Want you. Just once."

He laughed, shook his head. "That's actually the point. Our annulment will be predicated on the fact that we never consummated the marriage. If we do this now, you can't get an annulment. You'll be forced to get a divorce. And you, with a divorce in your past, won't be allowed to reign."

She stared at him, as if she'd actually forgotten. Then she stepped away. "Oh."

Disappointment swelled inside him. For some damned reason or another he thought she'd say, "So what?"

"You never thought of that?"

She shook her head, then smoothed an errant strand of black hair off her face. "I'm kind of making a fool of myself, aren't I?"

He reached out, took her elbows and pulled her close again. "I'm the one in the wrong. I want you enough that I almost slipped." He admitted it because he couldn't stand to have her think that any of this was because she wasn't beautiful, sexy, special. She was. And he wanted her so much his whole body ached. He almost didn't know where he got the courage, the honor to say, "But I also like you too much to deny you of your destiny. I don't know what you're going to do as queen, but I know you well enough to realize that whatever you do it will be special, wonderful. Your country probably needs that."

Her eyes saddened into the soft blue that made his chest hurt. But he held his ground, and his breath.

Eva stared into his eyes, a million confusing truths racing through her brain. This was the unspoken reality of what happened to people with destinies. Alex hadn't said it. He didn't need to. It was all there in his eyes. People with destinies rarely got what they wanted. Duty, responsibility came first.

She cursed it, then reminded herself of all the feelings she'd had the day her dad had called. The horrible knowledge that she'd been overlooked. The intense desire to be part of the team that put her beloved country back together again.

Would she throw it all away for one night with a man she longed for? The first man she'd ever really wanted?

She swallowed. She'd thought the answer would be easy. Instead she stood frozen. How could she decide without a kiss? Without a touch?

Her lips tingled at the thought of another kiss. Her entire body exploded at the thought more of his touch.

Something must have changed in her expression because he pulled back. "Oh, you are temptation. But, no. I can't be the person who steals your destiny from you."

Her eyes clung to his. "There is one way."

His eyebrows rose.

"I know I told you I wouldn't force you to stay married…but what if we wanted to?"

"Stay married?"

She nodded.

He squeezed his eyes shut. "You have known me four weeks. I can't ask for a life commitment after four weeks."

"But you were willing to marry a princess you didn't know."

"And now I know her and now I know she deserves more. Real love. Trust. A man who doesn't have walls."

He turned her in the direction of her room. "Go before I can't be noble anymore."

The next morning, she met Alex in the sitting room of their yacht suite for breakfast, pretending nothing had happened. He'd said that she hadn't made a fool of herself, that he wanted her, and if the intense expression in his eyes had been anything to judge by, he had wanted her.

In some ways that made her happy. In others, it turned her heart inside out. The very fact that he couldn't consummate their marriage once again said he might like her, he might be attracted to her, but he didn't want her forever.

Still, what did she expect? Everlasting love after four weeks? That was silly. And if there was one thing she'd realized she wasn't, it was silly.

So she put on shorts and a T-shirt, combed her hair but really didn't fix it. It might not be a real honeymoon, but it was a vacation. Then she sat at the small table with Alex.

Without looking up from the newspaper

he was reading, he said, "I didn't know what you'd want so I asked the staff to bring a bit of everything."

She laughed and the paper fell. Obviously, he'd been waiting for a sign that she didn't hate him.

How could she hate him for sticking to a deal she'd agreed to?

So she smiled.

He carefully returned her smile. "What do we want to do today?"

"I got word two days ago that my stipend was in my bank account. I need to get money to my shelters. But I was also hoping to have time to make phone calls to all the managers."

"That's what you want to do when you have an entire yacht at your disposal?"

"I haven't spoken to them in weeks. I need to catch up."

"All business on our honeymoon?"

"I'm sorry."

He folded the paper. "No. No. Don't be sorry. The staff assigned to our suite is made up of our most loyal personnel. They won't breathe a word of the fact that we don't sleep together. So, they won't bat an eye if you spend our first day on the phone handling business."

"It's okay then?"

"Yes, but tomorrow we should do something together."

"I don't water ski or do any of the daredevil sports you like."

He laughed. "That might be a good thing. The whole purpose of all this is to keep you alive."

She smiled. "Okay. So tomorrow we'll sit on deck chairs and read."

"Sounds good."

It really didn't sound good to Eva. It sounded like another chance in her life passing her by. She'd never make love to her first love.

It was the price she'd pay to be a queen. The price he'd pay to protect her.

And for the hundredth time, she wished the old Alex, the Alex who didn't care about royalty and responsibility, would swoop in and save her. Sweep her off her feet, make her glad to give up the crown.

But that was stupid…wasn't it?

CHAPTER TWELVE

THE MOOD IN the palace was celebratory when Alex and Eva arrived home two weeks later. Everyone had gathered in the king's quarters to greet them, so they headed there first.

Her mom enveloped her in a huge hug, a hug to rival one of Rose's hugs, and Eva laughed. "I see the Sancho family is rubbing off on you."

Karen took a glass of wine from King Ronaldo who was enjoying an afternoon of playing bartender.

Eva turned to Alex and whispered, "Your dad's in a weird mood."

Alex watched him mixing a martini for Rose. "I have a vague memory of him liking the job of bartender." He frowned. "If I'm remembering correctly, I think that's how he played host—"

He stopped abruptly. Eva wound her hand around his upper arm. She waited until he looked at her before she said, "Before your mom died."

His face shifted as if something had clicked into place for him. "It's so amazing to see him becoming himself again."

Just as it was probably amazing for the king to watch Alex become the prince he was always meant to be. Eva didn't say it, but pride for Alex surged through her, along with the abysmal realization that this family she was becoming a part of, this man she was so in love with, would soon be gone.

She pulled in a breath. "You know what? I'm a little bit tired. Do you mind if I go back to my quarters."

Alex whispered, "You can't go back to your quarters. We're married now. Staff will have already moved your things to mine."

"Oh." And the break she was hoping for flitted away.

"It's no big deal. We'll figure out how to handle it."

"Yes." She straightened her shoulders. "I'm sure we will."

"I can walk you back now."

She looked away. "I can find my own way, remember? I've been there for plenty of pretend lunches and suppers."

She knew that sounded bitter, so she faced him and said, "Sorry. I'm just very tired and getting a headache. Let me go get settled. You enjoy your time with family."

He nodded but walked her to the door of his father's quarters. He said, "Maybe you should take a nap."

She said, "Sure. That's probably what I'll do."

As she turned to walk away, she noticed Alex motioning to one of the guards to follow her to the apartment, and suddenly she was very, very tired.

She entered Alex's apartment, working not to remember the casual dinners they'd shared where she'd slowly but surely fallen in love with him.

Given that the staff believed they were married for real, she knew that her things were in Alex's closet, so she walked to her room deciding she could take a nap in her camisole and panties. She wouldn't be so bold as to walk into the man's closet when he wasn't there. Worse, his bedroom. She didn't want to see if he was tidy or messy. She didn't want to see his toothbrush and shaving creams. They'd already done too many personal, intimate things. Too many things she'd have to forget when they parted. She didn't need more reminders of everything she was losing. She just wanted all of this to be over.

On the way to her bedroom, she kicked off her sandals. She yanked her sweater over her head and it fell from her tired fingers. She stopped long enough to slide her jeans to the floor and step out of them. Some little voice in the back of her head told her to pick up the jeans, pick up the trail of clothes she was leaving, but a heaviness consumed her. She barely got to the bed before she crumbled, luckily landing face-first on the mattress.

From the way his dad and Rose, and Ginny and Dom behaved, Alex would have thought they believed he and Eva were actually married. He knew part of this was for the benefit of the charade. But, really? Sometimes his dad and Rose just got carried away. They loved family.

Twenty minutes later, with Rose still regaling them with stories from her days as a public school teacher in Texas, Alex looked at his watch. He'd known Eva had needed some space. He didn't blame her. Though they'd spent their days on the yacht resting, reading, watching glorious sunsets, it was wearing to pretend to be honeymooning when they would go back to their suite and sleep in separate rooms.

But this afternoon there'd been something a little different in her eyes. Something more than exhaustion. So he gave Rose's hilarious stories another ten minutes, then excused himself and headed for his quarters.

He saw the trail of clothes to her room and burst out laughing.

"Very funny, Eva."

He picked up the first shoe, then the second. Took a few steps and grabbed her sweater. Another few steps and he could scoop up her jeans. He turned to open the door of her bedroom but it was already open, and Eva lay, facefirst, on the soft comforter of the queen-sized bed.

He laughed. "That's a weird way to take a nap." But as he walked into the room darkened by thick drapes, he realized she was in nothing but panties and a camisole. Silky white with a wide lace border.

He stopped. Cleared his throat. Obviously she was sleeping, so he'd just drop her jeans, sweater and shoes on a chair in the back. He walked past the bed, dumped the clothes, and turned to leave the room, but as he approached the bed, he noticed her breathing was labored, difficult.

He walked over. "Eva?"

She didn't move.

He bent and nudged her shoulder. "Eva?"

She still didn't move.

He grabbed the receiver from the palace phone by her bed. "This is Alex. Send a doctor to my quarters immediately."

It seemed to take forever for the doctor to arrive with a nurse, but the second they rang the bell, he opened the door.

Alex had turned on the overhead light, pulled back the covers and shifted her on the bed so that she was lying on her back.

When he took the doctor to her room, it was easy to see the bright red splotches on her cheeks. Her head shifted on the pillow. She moaned as if in pain.

Dr. Martin looped his stethoscope around his neck. "I can see from here that she's got a fever." He walked over to the bed, took a look at her face and turned to Alex. "I'm going to have Sarah take her vitals." He motioned Alex to the door and walked him out of the room and up the hall.

"After Sarah gets the vitals, I'll have a look

at her. We'll also need to draw some blood for tests."

Alex said, "Okay."

"Do you want me to call Dom to come and sit with you?"

"No. I'm fine."

The doctor smiled. "Okay. Great." He headed down the hall, but faced Alex again. "You know I have to report this visit to your dad, right?"

Alex nodded. Didn't every flipping thing they did have to be reported?

"Great. Blood tests will take a few hours. Are you sure you don't want somebody called?"

He nodded, realizing that the person he'd want called to help him through an afternoon of waiting was Eva. But she was the one who was sick.

When Dr. Martin and Sarah came out of her room after the exam, he asked, "Can I go in and sit with her?"

Dr. Martin winced. "Actually, Alex, you risk catching the flu. I can't be certain, but it looks like that's what she picked up. Maybe from someone on the yacht."

"Which means I've already been exposed."

The doctor shrugged. "I'd prefer you stay away. If you want someone with her, I can send up nurses who will do twenty-four-hour shifts."

A sudden memory of his mom being sick sprang into his head. He remembered his dad by her side twenty-four hours a day and suddenly understood why.

"I'll take the risk."

"I have to report this to your father."

"So you said."

The doctor sighed and left with Sarah the nurse and Alex walked back to her room.

She was under the covers, dressed in a pair of pajamas. Alex had no idea where they'd come from, but all Doc had to do was get on the phone and tell someone in housekeeping to send pajamas and they'd probably be delivered through the back door.

He walked to the bed, not liking Eva's labored breathing, but knowing she was being cared for by one of the best. Crouching at the side of the bed, he pushed her hair off her forehead and wished that they'd met under different circumstances.

Because wishing accomplished nothing, he forced himself to his feet, but didn't leave her room. He pulled a Queen Anne chair from a corner of the room to the side of the bed. When he fell asleep, it was only for a few minutes at a time. So he crawled onto her bed. He stretched out beside her and fell asleep for a few hours, but when he woke up she was thrashing. The second he touched her hand, she stopped. So he stayed, right where he was, not under the covers, on top. Sometimes he'd smooth her hair from her face. For the most part he just held her hand. Until she scooted closer and snuggled against him. He wrapped his arms around her and slept. Not for long stretches, but longer than he might have slept on that uncomfortable chair.

In the morning, the doctor ordered him to go to bed and he told the old grouch that he'd go as soon as the doctor's visit was over.

But he didn't leave. He stayed in the chair, watching her. Though the temptation was strong to lie on the bed with her, he resisted it. He watched nurses take her temperature, wake her up enough to give her meds and even cool her head with a wet cloth.

When the doctor returned that evening it was to announce that her fever had broken.

"Now, there's no reason to sit by her bed. You can get some sleep."

He walked the old man to the door, and hesitated at the place where he'd go left to his own room, or right to Eva's.

But staying in her room was silly. She was over the worst of it now. And he needed some sleep.

He turned left, got a shower and shrugged into a T-shirt and a pair of pajama pants. But when he lifted the cover off his bed, he couldn't slide inside.

For some reason or another, he simply could not leave her alone. He knew she only had the flu. He knew her fever had broken. But he just couldn't leave her by herself in a room that was unfamiliar to her.

Still, he was tired. Exhausted. So he walked to the empty side of her bed, lifted the cover and slid inside. When she turned to him, he wrapped his arms around her. The second he closed his eyes, he fell asleep.

When Eva awakened she had no idea what time it was…or what day. Vague images passed through her brain but nothing stuck. She was also comfortably tucked against someone. Not the way a mother or father cradles a child, but closer.

Alex.

Some of the images gelled in her mind. Him ordering around a man in a gray suit. Him giving uniformed nurses instructions.

She smiled.

"Go back to sleep. You might have slept away the past thirty-six hours. But I've slept in fits and starts."

On this bed. With her. Flashes of him lying beside her, stroking her hair, flitted to her. That's why his arms around her hadn't awakened her. He'd done this before. Maybe even the entire night before.

She stilled her hands at her sides and felt silky material.

"The nurses did that. Changed your PJs twice. They also gave you two sponge baths. Though I volunteered, they shot me down."

She laughed.

"There you go. Now I know you're not just awake, you're feeling better."

"I am."

"Well, go back to sleep. It's still night. And I'm tired."

He was staying? Was he going to hold her the entire time he slept?

Happiness overwhelmed her and suddenly she felt every inch of him that touched her. Not just his warmth, but the softness of a T-shirt and cotton sleep pants. His bicep was her pillow. Her cheek rested against his chest. It was the most intimate, most wonderful feeling.

"Don't ever do that again."

His voice filtered to her softly, filled with a casual intimacy that caused joy to radiate to every nook and cranny of her body.

"Do what?"

"Get so sick that half the palace worried you were going to die, or that we'd put so much stress on you we'd killed you."

She carefully, slowly raised her hand until she could lay it against his chest. Not so much out of curiosity about what he felt like, but more out of a longing to know what it felt like to be allowed to touch him.

"All I remember is a headache."

"You had a virus."

Here they were, apparently in the middle of the night, having a conversation while wrapped in each other's arms. She flattened her palm against his chest, reveled in the steady rhythm of his breathing, knew this was what being married felt like: a quiet, unspoken connection.

"A weak virus if I've only been sleeping thirty-six hours."

"Strong enough that your mother almost sent for clergy."

She laughed and snuggled against him. His arms tightened around her. "I seem to remember you bossing around the nurses."

"I have a marriage license that says I can."

She suppressed a smile. "So you're one of those types who throw their weight around."

"I haven't spent six weeks protecting you only to have a virus kill you."

He said it so easily, as if that was all it was, but his muscles tightened.

She suddenly wished she could see his face, see the naked emotion in his dark, dark eyes. But then she'd have to pull away. It wasn't often he let her be so close, let her touch him, let himself touch her.

"You like me."

He laughed. "Of course, I like you."

"No. You *like* me."

He stilled. The room got very quiet.

"Does it matter?"

It mattered to her. A great deal. If only because her heart needed to know. Needed to hear him say that something had blossomed between them, because she couldn't take another day of being so close to him, yet being emotionally separated.

"It matters."

"Then, yes. I have feelings for you that I shouldn't have."

"I have feelings for you too." Such an inadequate description of the emotions that squeezed her heart and captured her soul. Made her hot and cold. Made her long to be with him as he distanced herself from her. Made her understand the bond between her parents that was strong enough that her dad could pretend to leave with a mistress and trust her mother would collapse into his arms when the truth was revealed. She almost couldn't bear the strength of it… Yet it slipped out as one tiny sentence.

His voice was slow, hesitant as he said, "I know."

Her heart tripped over itself in her chest. It wasn't the first time they'd talked about this. But it was the first time she believed they could both be honest. "I—"

"Go to sleep, Princess."

She heard the tiredness in his voice. Felt his muscles relaxing as if he were drifting off and wanted to shout, "No! I need this." But she didn't. She didn't say anything else and soon she knew from his relaxed body that he was asleep.

She awakened the next morning to find him gone. She slid her hand along the space where he'd slept. It was cold.

Hopelessness billowed through her. She'd had her moment, but it was gone.

She showered and dressed in jeans and a top, not quite sure what her mother would have planned for the day, but knowing she needed to spend time with her mom to make up for their fourteen-day separation.

Expecting to find Alex's quarters empty, she stopped short when she walked in on him in his small dining room, eating breakfast. He rose when he saw her and came over to pull her chair away from the table. But before he let her sit, he took her shoulders and looked into her eyes.

"Don't ever scare me like that again."

The crazy feeling of intimacy from the night before trembled through her. "I won't."

He kissed her cheek then sniffed a laugh as he returned to his own seat. "You just promised you'll never get the flu?"

His words slid through her, as she sat. He said it as if they would be together forever. The hope that had died tried to flicker to life. She swallowed.

"I should have gotten the vaccination."

"You should have." He frowned when she reached for a platter of eggs. "You might want to go easy on food today, give your body a chance to recover."

"I'm ravenous. Besides, the flu is gone. I was better last night when we—"

She couldn't say snuggled. She wanted to. But she couldn't even say slept together, even though sleep was all they did. Silly superstition filled her. Almost as if she was afraid that if she said any of it out loud, she'd jinx it.

He caught her gaze. "Had our chat?"

"Yes."

He rose from his seat. Tossing his napkin to the table, he walked over to her, bent down and kissed her cheek. "I have things to do this morning, but don't make plans for lunch. If your stomach really is up to it, we'll go see Angelo."

Her body went soft, almost boneless, over the wonderful intimacy that hadn't disappeared as she'd believed it would.

On the way to the door, he stopped a maid. "My wife is better this morning. But I don't want to take any chances with germs. Clean her room as if the royal health inspectors will be visiting."

Eva laughed. He spun to face her. "You laugh. But you don't know what a scare you gave me."

"Over the flu?"

He said, "Over something," then left the apartment.

Eva sat very still. The only other "something" in that equation had been the possibility that he'd lose her.

The hope flickering in her roared into a flame of possibility. Would he eventually realize that he'd lose her when her father returned? Would he stop her?

After a morning spent with his brother and father, catching up on everything that had happened while he was gone, Alex was glad he'd made lunch plans with Eva. The two weeks they'd been away had been quiet. Dom was even shaving back the amount of time he spent helping Eva's dad. Soon, King Mason would be returning to rule. He'd upend his country; that was for sure. But the changes would be for the better.

Everybody was happy. Especially Alex. Eva had scared him beyond belief with a simple case of the flu. But she was well now. And he couldn't shake the out-of-proportion happiness that brought. She'd had the flu, not the plague. Yet every time he looked at her and saw the light in her eyes, the color in her cheeks, crazy pleasure flooded him.

It was weird.

He hoped lunch with her would get him beyond it. Except she wore a pretty blue top that made her eyes look even bluer and Angelo didn't just make lunch. He sat with them, telling Eva stories of when Alex was at university and he'd sneak the private plane to come home and have dinner at Angelo's.

"Just because I could," Alex said, shaking his head.

Angelo tapped Eva's hand. "He was drunk with power."

Eva laughed but Alex straightened. "I wasn't drunk with power as much as I was experimenting with my power."

Catching his gaze, Eva said, "Ah. I get it now."

And he felt it again. That fluttery happiness that was more than relief that she was well. It was as if somebody turned on a light in a very dark room.

He got up from his chair. "Angelo, the next time we come here, I want to vet the stories you decide to tell."

The old chef laughed merrily. "What fun would that be?"

"Are you trying to get my wife to run for the hills?"

"No. I'm telling her the stories before she hears them from strangers." Angelo rose as

Alex helped Eva stand. "Look at it this way, if I tell them in front of you, then you have a chance to defend yourself."

"Good point."

He took Eva's hand. She smiled at him. As they made their way to his Mercedes, body-guards shifted and scrambled. They all seemed a little too alert, more alert than they had just two hours ago when they'd driven to the res-taurant.

He told himself he was imagining it.

"Can I drive?"

He glanced at Eva as he reached into his pocket for the keys, but Jeffrey, today's team leader, walked over.

He bowed. "Prince, allow me the honor of driving."

Alex handed him the keys. He knew better than to argue. Something had happened.

But he didn't get an inkling of a word about it when he left Eva in their apartment and went to his father's office and Dom's. Both were out at meetings and no one on either staff seemed to know what was going on.

When he asked Jeffrey, all he said was, "Your father implemented a secondary pro-tocol which we followed. I assumed it was a test or a dry run since we've had no threats."

"A dry run?"

"We do them all the time."

And wouldn't it make sense that his father would want his bodyguards preparing for the day when Eva's father returned.

His gut tightened. Though he tried to tell himself it was out of fear, he realized it was because he would miss her.

When he finally returned to the apartment, Eva stood in the sitting room wearing a slim red dress.

His eyebrows rose. "Going somewhere?"

"We're all having dinner." She pointed to her dress. "Semiformal, with your dad and Rose, Dom and Ginny and my mom."

"So no tux?"

She shrugged. "I'm not entirely sure. You never know with Rose."

"Maybe I can get away with nice trousers and a dinner jacket."

"Do you feel lucky?"

He laughed. "Are you quoting American movies to me?"

"An old one. Go. You have about ten minutes before we have to leave."

He showered quickly and though he looked at a tux, he decided on a simple jacket and trousers. His day might have been calm and casual by Dom's standards, but it wasn't easy to get back into the swing of working. Especially not when he'd spent the afternoon thinking something was up, only to discover his cause for alarm had only been something like a fire drill.

When he met Eva in the sitting room, she walked over and straightened his collar. "There. Now you're perfect."

The strange sensation he kept getting around her filled him, then grew.

He shook his head to clear it of the feeling and motioned her to the door. "We have about a minute and a half left then we're late and Rose hates it when anybody's late."

"My mom does too."

He stopped her at the door, before they would have been in public space where someone could have overheard. "How's she holding up, by the way?"

"Now that she knows the truth, she's like a kid at Christmas. She's proud that she did her job and eager to see her husband again."

He said, "That's good." But a weird empathy rippled along the edges of his skin. He'd decided it was because they'd all had a part to play. So of course, he understood Karen's feelings.

But after a long elaborate dinner that seemed more like a celebration, Alex walked Eva to their apartment in silence.

He didn't even want to think that the so-called fire drill this morning had been practice for possible trouble when her dad made his announcements about the plot to oust him. He didn't want to think tonight's dinner had been a goodbye dinner for Eva and her mom.

That would mean she was leaving the next day, and he just didn't want to think about it.

He opened the apartment door and directed Eva to walk in before him. She stepped into the sitting room, removing her earrings.

"That was unexpectedly nice."

"Yes. It was."

She faced him with a smile. "Your father found a real gem when he found Rose."

"Technically, Dad didn't find Rose. Dom brought her here to help Ginny adjust."

She walked over to him, her head angled to the right, a silly smile on her full lips. "I'm guessing that was a great story."

"It was. What I know of it, at least. I'm not privy to all the private stuff, but Dom very honestly admits he simply couldn't resist Ginny."

"The power of love."

Gazing into Eva's silvery blue eyes, he almost believed it. But it didn't matter. She had a destiny and he wasn't ruining that for her. She, at least, needed the chance to decide who she was. To go home, as herself, to figure out what role she wanted to fill in her kingdom.

But what he wouldn't give for one night.

She bounced her earrings in her hand. "I guess I'll go to bed."

He stepped back. "Yeah. Me too."

But she didn't move. And the temptation that rocked him almost pushed him over the edge. She was beautiful, soft, smart, elegant and poised, yet delightfully normal. And the law said she was his.

But she wasn't a private jet that he could commandeer, use and return. And he wasn't a kid anymore, who took what he wanted without consideration for the consequences.

Though it felt like an actual, physical pain when he forced his legs to move, to walk away from her, he did.

CHAPTER THIRTEEN

ALEX WAS IN parliament the next day when one of his secretaries stealthily entered and slid a note into his hands.

The news has broken that Prince Gerard of Grennady has been arrested. King Mason is in your father's office. Your presence is requested.

He bounced out of his seat, caught Dom's gaze, then nudged his head in the direction of the door. Dom gave a quick, curt nod.

Alex exited calmly, but once in the high-ceilinged foyer, he began to run. He wasn't sure why. He had no idea where the sense of urgency came from. But he had a picture in his head of King Mason loading his wife and daughter into a helicopter or plane and Eva waving goodbye from a window—

And he'd never see her again.

Wouldn't even get a proper goodbye.

He ran faster. His heart was pounding, his breaths shallow and uneven until he reached the secretary's office outside his father's door.

He stopped, leveled his breathing and, without asking permission from the secretary, opened his father's office door and stepped inside.

"Here's the man of the hour now," his father boomed. He, King Mason, Rose, Karen and Eva stood in a cluster in front of his desk. There was no silver tea service with coffee and scones on the low table in front of the sofa in the conversation area in the corner. There was no sigh of relief, no relaxing on the overstuffed chairs. No one sat. Everyone stood, as if the King of Grennady was eager to be off.

"I've never seen anyone step up the way Alex did." When Alex reached his father, he clapped Alex on the back. "The wedding was perfect. No one would have ever believed the two of them weren't in love."

Alex's gaze snapped to Eva's. Her eyes were red-rimmed as if she'd had a tearful reunion with her dad. When she smiled at Alex, her lips wobbled.

He held her gaze. He knew the past six

weeks had been difficult for her. But there had been joy in there too. A wedding. Stolen kisses. Confidences that had rocked his soul. "It's Eva who deserves the credit."

He wasn't the screw-up he had been when she arrived. The guy who lived for himself. He'd more than done his duty. He'd become the prince his father had always wished he would be.

Knowing her had made him who he was.

And now…

Right now…

His whole life was in her hands.

Except he didn't think he had the right to ask her to stay. She couldn't rule from Xaviera.

King Mason slid his arm around his daughter's shoulders. "I watched your news every day. She was magnificent. But I had no doubt that she would be." He smiled at her. "She'll be a queen one day." He looked over at Alex. "And you'd have made her a fine husband for real. I'm sorry we had to screw that up."

Alex glanced at Eva. No one, it seemed, realized something had happened between him and Eva.

He waited a heartbeat for her to say something. Anything. To ask him to come with her. Because that was their only option.

But King Mason said, "We really need to be going. This hit the press two hours ago and I need to get in front of my parliament."

Alex's dad shook Mason's hand. "You have your speech."

"I'll be refining it on the flight home."

Karen hugged Rose. "This might have been nothing but a charade but I think you're the best friend I've ever had. I hope we can get together."

Rose winked. "I think we need to do a little shopping in Paris."

Karen laughed. "I would love that."

Alex waited. Eva had missed the opportunity to tell her family that what she felt for Alex had been real. Hell, he'd let it go by too. Because it wasn't really his choice. It was hers. She'd asked him once to stay married to her, but he'd said no. He wouldn't steal her destiny. He couldn't change his mind now. Could he?

Eva hugged his dad. "Thank you."

"Princess, you were a delight. Anytime you feel like a beach vacation, you just fly down."

"I will."

Then she turned to him. Her eyes were bright, not filled with the hopeful, wistful look that had made him feel he could see the whole way to her soul. She was happy.

"Thank you, Prince Alex."

He sniffed a laugh. "I think that's the first time you've given me a title."

She held his gaze. "You earned it."

And he couldn't think of anything to say. He couldn't say, "Please stay." He couldn't pull her away from a country where she would be queen. He couldn't say, "I love you," because he wasn't sure he did. So he couldn't ask her for a little time to get to know each other—or date—because that seemed ridiculous.

But she could ask him.

Just ask.

Just say the word.

One word.

Any word.

She stepped forward and put her arms around him, hugging him awkwardly. He smelled her scented hair. Breathed in the scent, as his heart realized she wasn't going to say anything.

She pulled away.

And his heart did something he'd never felt before. Not even when Nina died.

It shattered.

"Goodbye, Alex."

"Goodbye, Eva." He meant for that to sound strong. Instead, his voice was hoarse, scratchy.

She turned to her parents, who gathered her up and walked through the door where members of the royal guard awaited them.

"They have to go five floors to the roof and run a good distance to their helicopter," Dominic said.

Alex whipped around to face him.

"You can catch her."

He blinked. He *could* catch her. He could stop her.

And tell her what?

Promise her what?

She would someday be a queen. She was strong. Smart. Capable.

What the hell would she want him around for?

But his father made a sound of distaste and said, "Never belabor goodbyes. Leave Eva with the memory of you strong. I'm sure you'll meet again, and you'll laugh about this. But right now I'm releasing you for a much deserved holiday."

The helicopter flight to the royal airstrip and Grennady's private jet was too noisy to talk and Eva was glad. She'd never felt this odd feeling. Almost as if she were outside her body, watching this happen to someone else.

She knew her dad coming home would be disruptive. Surprising. Totally out of the blue. Especially for her mom, who was so desperate to see him, to know that he really was still hers. But it wasn't seeing her dad that left Eva feeling as if she were vibrating with confusion.

It was leaving Alex.

It was being there in that room, almost begging him with her eyes to admit to their families that they'd become close for real, and having him step back, away from her, that caused her stomach to fall and her nerve endings to shimmy.

She'd thought he was beginning to see that they belonged together but apparently she'd been wrong.

The helicopter landed and they ran to the plane. As soon as they were inside the main cabin, her mom put her hands on both of Eva's cheeks and kissed her soundly.

"You have definitely proven yourself. You are Grennady's next queen."

She tried to smile.

"Yes. Your mother is right. I realized while watching you every day that you weren't just the woman who'd bear our next heir," her dad said, hugging her one more time. "You were made to rule."

She sniffed a laugh. "I realized it too. Actually, Alex realized it first." Saying the sentence out loud, picturing the times and the ways he'd said it, slowed her heartbeat. Their relationship had always seemed so real to her because some of it was. He'd been her friend. Her partner in their charade. And eventually he'd grown to like her.

How could something that real be over in the space of what seemed like seconds?

She almost said something, but her mom began talking about her having a real reign and her dad began enumerating things she'd have to do, like get daily briefings and attend parliament when it was in session, maybe take over a committee or two.

She nodded and smiled, thrilled for the opportunity, but she couldn't stop thinking about Alex.

Actually, what she probably needed was time alone.

But her parents went on discussing her reign through the plane ride with Eva participating as much as she could. Her dad wanted her on the dais with him at the press conference the following day. But he wanted her to wait to actually introduce herself into parliament until after he'd totally settled things. This was a point in his reign when he needed to look strong and though having her at his side was good, a king had to be autonomous. When she was queen, there'd probably come a time when she'd have to do the same thing. Stand alone, as a leader. Someone their subjects could trust.

When they arrived in Grennady, their airstrip was quiet, deserted. The drive to their palace was still, though the air hummed with the realization that her dad had a lot of work to do. As soon as they arrived, he walked directly to parliament.

Her mom went to her quarters to lie down and Eva spent some time on her bed too. But she couldn't sleep. She couldn't anything. Her mind was numb. She was so filled with sorrow and confusion that she couldn't even close her eyes.

Engaged in the duty of pulling his country together again, her dad didn't come home for dinner. Eva met her mom in the private dining room in her parents' quarters. But she didn't eat. She stared at the food as if it was a foreign object.

"Sweetie?"

Her head snapped up. "What?"

"I was just about to ask you the same thing. What's wrong?"

"I think I'm just having a little trouble adjusting. This time yesterday I was married—" She stopped herself. "Pretending to be married. Then suddenly Dad was in King Ronaldo's office and we were on a helicopter."

Her mom's eyes narrowed as she studied Eva's face. "It did all happen fast."

"No warning," Eva agreed. "No time to prepare."

"What would you have had to prepare? You were in on the plan. You knew that at any moment your dad would come to Xaviera to get us and take us home."

Eva cleared her throat. "That's the way it was in the beginning. But the pretending went on so long." She sucked in a breath. Closed her eyes. "I got married, Mom."

"As part of a charade," her mom reminded her. Then her face changed. "Wait." She gasped. "You didn't—"

"No. We *didn't*."

"Well, thank God for that because if I'm reading this right that's your basis for an annulment."

"Yes."

"And you need an annulment, not a divorce if you want to be queen."

The dining room got quiet. Karen ate a few

bites, but glanced at Eva again. "Are you sure you're okay?"

Eva nodded.

Her mom sighed. "Tomorrow, you will have to go in front of the press to answer questions and with the knowledge that you won't just be a placeholder. Your father saw your strength. He knows you can rule and he will be telling the country that tomorrow. You can't be this—" She fumbled for a word and finally settled on, "Quiet."

"I'll be fine tomorrow."

Her mother studied Eva's face again. "You're sure?"

"Yes."

"And there's nothing you want to talk about?"

She would have loved to have talked. But as her mother said, she was a woman who would someday be a queen. Anytime she fell apart, had doubts, was human, she would be perceived as weak. And she'd seen firsthand that her uncle's family, the ones next in line for the throne, would exploit that.

So she couldn't talk. Except to a confidant… like a husband who understood. Like Alex.

She licked her suddenly dry lips. He hadn't asked her to stay, hadn't told their families that the charade had turned to real love—probably because for him, it hadn't. And he had a real life to get back to. Their charade had changed him. He had duties, responsibilities now.

Truth wore away some of her shock and created a struggle inside of her. The woman who loved him wanted to weep. The woman who would be queen put her shoulders back and recognized her duty.

But in bed that night, the tears came and she realized she'd finally had her heart broken. And if this pain, this sorrow, this anguish, was anything to go by, Alex must have suffered a thousand times over when he lost his first love, the woman who kept him from wanting to love again.

The next day, she and her father were in front of the press, explaining the entire charade.

At the end, when a cheeky reporter asked her if she hadn't, even once, wished her marriage to Xaviera's handsome Playboy Prince was real, she'd shaken her head with a laugh and said, "Absolutely not. I was doing my duty."

Alex stared at the TV in his father's office, watching the closed circuit TV feed that Grennady had provided the rulers of Xaviera who would most assuredly be contacted for comments.

Eva wore a red suit—the color recommended to all leaders when they wanted to show their power. Her soft blue eyes were sharp today. Her gaze was clear, direct. Her chin was high. Her shoulders were back. Her comments were short, emotionless. Even as she demonstrated she would not steal her father's thunder, she wore all the marks of a queen.

When she said, "Absolutely not. I was doing my duty," his muscles froze. He told them not to. He reminded them he should have expected this.

But he pictured her on the yacht, eating dinner with him in the moonlight.

He saw her in the wedding dress.

He remembered holding her the night she was sick, when he all but admitted he had feelings for her.

And he saw past the future queen to the woman she'd buried somewhere inside her.

He knew that woman was weeping.

But he also knew he was out. She didn't need him.

His chest hurt and he rubbed it, the way he used to when he thought of Nina. Funny, he hadn't even had an inkling of a memory of her in weeks. Not once.

Rose peered over at him from the leather couch in the corner. "You okay, sweet pea?"

He grabbed a breath of air, giving himself a second to make sure he looked and sounded normal. "Yes. I'm fine."

The king rose from the oversized chair in front of the TV. "Of course he's fine. He's better than fine. He should be proud of himself. His changes to security details and eye for finding the loopholes might have saved Eva's life." He glanced at his watch. "Aren't you scheduled to be on the jet in a few minutes?"

"Yes." He was. Though his father had told him he could leave yesterday he hadn't been able to figure out where to go. This morning, he'd booked the royal family's jet to take him to the United States. He loved New York, but he wasn't going there for the restaurants or the shows. He wanted to see Eva's shelters. It filled him with pain to admit it. But he just couldn't take the sudden goodbye. Yet he also knew he couldn't just fly to her country and expect her to see him. He just wanted another day or two to get adjusted to the fact that she was out of his life, and her cats were about as close to her as he would get.

Then he'd be fine. He'd force himself to be fine.

He tried a smile, reached way down in his soul until he found the frivolous personality that had served him so well for decades.

"I haven't been to the US in a long time. I'm sure Vegas has missed me."

Dom slapped his back. "You enjoy yourself."

The king snorted. "If you hadn't earned this, I'd be a bit angry that you booked four weeks. You have duties now. When I told you that you could go I was thinking more like a week."

And Alex laughed. Because he knew he was supposed to. "Right. But I'm thinking I earned a little longer. I'll see you all next month."

He headed for the door, but Rose suddenly popped up from the sofa. "I'll walk you to your apartment."

He frowned. He hadn't needed someone to walk him anywhere in decades. But he didn't argue. Frivolous Alex rarely argued. "Sure. Great."

Their heels clicked on the marble floor of the corridors that took them to the elevator to his wing.

When the doors closed, Rose faced him. She didn't say a word. She just stared into his eyes.

"What?"

"You miss her."

"Of course, I miss her. She's a good person. She was a good sport about the charade. We spent a lot of time together. And I thought we'd become friends."

"Did it irritate you that she didn't even blink when they asked her if she'd gotten feelings for you?"

He picked imaginary lint off his jacket sleeve. "No."

She caught his hand to stop it. "Oh, sweetie. It's worse than I thought. You love her."

"I loved two women in my life. They both died." He faked a smile but thinking about them no longer hurt. His mom and Nina felt like part of his distant past with no place in his future except for memories of happy times. But Eva had been in his present for weeks. She had given him more happy times, more fun, more of a sense of purpose than he'd ever had, but he'd known she was going. Hell, he wanted her to go. He wanted her to fulfill her destiny. Yes, he was a bit sad, but he'd visit her shelters, suck it up and move on. Because that's what he did.

"Wouldn't I be a fool to fall for someone I *knew* would be taken away?"

To his chagrin, Rose laughed. "Seriously?

You think I'm going to buy that. I did not fall off a turnip truck yesterday."

"Turnip truck?"

She batted a hand. "Never mind. It's a saying we have in Texas. It sort of means I'm too smart to believe what you're saying. My point is you can kid your dad and maybe even Dom for a while, but I see all the signs."

"You see nothing."

"Exactly. A guy who'd only been in the charade to do his duty would be preening about his success. You're too damned quiet."

"That doesn't mean I love her." He tossed Rose his most charming smile. "I'm not the kind of guy to settle down, remember?"

She shook her head. "I'm not buying that stupid smile either."

"Oh, chill. Being the happy-go-lucky prince is my place."

She shook her head. "That's baloney."

"Baloney? A luncheon meat?"

"Sorry. It's another thing we say in the US." She stopped, took his hands and looked into his eyes. "When the chips were down, you stepped in. And for the six weeks Eva was under intense pressure, you supported her."

"So?"

"So you're different. Very different. You

took charge of her protection. Scrutinized her security details. Had a say in every route she took."

He said nothing. He knew he was different. They all knew he was different. But he could be responsible Alex in four weeks. Right now, he wanted his time off.

"You didn't just love her enough to take care of her; you loved her."

When he didn't reply, she sighed.

"You can't tell me you don't see it."

Anger whooshed through him. "All right. I see it! Damn it. But everybody I've ever loved has been taken from me. Why in the hell would I deliberately connect with or commit to someone whose very title makes her a target?"

Rose's features softened. "You're afraid."

"It doesn't matter."

"Of course, it does when your fear is unfounded. Your father told me Lieutenant Carver told him you were the most naturally gifted strategist he'd ever seen. You could spot a hole in a security detail that looked airtight. You came up with some of their best strategies." She nudged his arm. "Did you ever stop to think that makes you perfect for her? She's a tiny woman with a big future, and she leaned on you and you were there for her. Now she's a tiny woman with a big future who has no one."

He sucked in a long breath. "All of this is pointless. While she was here, she thought she loved me. Now that she's home, I'm barely a footnote in a press conference."

To his surprise, Rose laughed. "She's a future queen. She will never let herself look weak in public. But don't forget, you let her walk away."

He drew in a breath as an avalanche of thoughts tumbled down on him. She didn't wear her heart on her sleeve. She would be a strong ruler. And she did love him. "She does love me."

Rose smiled. "Yeah. She does. And she needs you."

He pulled his fingers through his hair. "I should have admitted my feelings when her dad returned."

Rose batted a hand. "No. You shouldn't have. You needed to think it through. Plus, you don't want your declaration of love to be public. You want this to be private. This time, you're not two royals fulfilling the terms of a treaty. She is a woman and you are the man who loves her. This needs to be done privately. It has to be done correctly."

CHAPTER FOURTEEN

IT TOOK TWO weeks for the furor over the assassination plot to die down. Another week for Grennady's royal family to be seen in public, proving the threat had been neutralized and they were back in control. Week four, Eva's dad sent her to the US, to her projects—as he called them. She might be next in line to the throne but he was king now. He wanted it to look like things were back to normal.

So she left. Though she would be briefed every morning, via video call, so she could take over in a moment's notice if need be, she would essentially be going back to living her life the way she had pre-threat. Pre-Alex.

She could think about him now without getting tears in her eyes. She hadn't told her mom. She hadn't told her friends. She hadn't told anyone that she loved him, that she'd fallen for a charade because that wasn't what future queens did.

Future queens were always strong.

But in America, where everyone knew who she was, but no one cared, she could be whatever she wanted. She could have a few glasses of wine with friends who let her be her. She could go to nightclubs. She could browse bookstores. She could stay in her apartment twenty-four-seven. Whatever she needed, she could do. Even if she wanted to sit in Central Park and cry, the new bodyguards assigned to her were sworn to secrecy.

She drove her nondescript little car up to a shelter she'd created in a New York City borough and parked. Her bodyguards in the SUV parked across the street. She'd decided to live her life exactly as she always had pre-threat. Instead of her new detail of bodyguards driving her, she'd taken a page from Alex's book and had them drive behind her. Always there but out of the way.

Thinking of Alex made her close her eyes and draw a long, deep breath. Her six weeks with him had been the most intense, yet somehow fun weeks of her life. Of course, he'd impacted her. Of course, she'd remember things.

But eventually the memories would fade. That's what she had to cling to.

She stepped out of the car and walked to the

old building that had once been a florist shop. When she opened the door, two tabbies and a tortoiseshell cat raced over. They wrapped around her ankles, not trying to get out, but looking for love.

She picked up the tortoiseshell. "Hey, Sophie. Still here I see." The cat nuzzled her face. Basking in the warmth of the cat's affection, the first hint of normalcy returned.

Angela, the shelter manager, raced out from the back room and over to Eva. "Oh, my God! I thought that was your voice." She hugged her fiercely, squishing the tortie between them, then she pulled back and looked Eva in the eye. "Someone tried to kill you?"

Eva laughed. After four weeks, it was possible to laugh about a plot that had been foiled. She scratched behind Sophia's ears. "There was a plot but we stopped it."

"With the help of another royal family. And a fake wedding where you looked gorgeous, by the way." She sighed eloquently. "So dreamy."

She wasn't surprised the entire story had reached the US. Royal gossip was royal gossip. Everybody loved it. But she couldn't think of the Sancho family or the wedding without getting a ping of pain in her heart. And it was time to move on.

"Dreamy is in the eye of the beholder."

"So what was he like? The prince?"

"He was doing his duty." And she wasn't quite as ready to talk about this as she had thought. She smiled. "So what's going on here?"

Angela walked behind the counter. "I'd rather hear about the prince, but if you insist on talking shop, you're the boss." She lifted some papers from beside the cash register. "We were able to stave off creditors until you got some money to us."

"I'm so sorry that I forgot you."

"If my calculations are correct, the slip was right before your wedding." She laughed gaily. "I still can't believe you got married."

"Fake married," she reminded Angela. "What else?"

"Same old. Same old," Angela said, then she brightened. "But we did get a new volunteer."

"Really?"

Angela leaned across the counter and whispered, "He's gorgeous."

"Gorgeous doesn't matter. Ability with cats does. And why are you whispering?"

"He's here. In the back. Doing chores."

"Oh."

Angela bounced from behind the counter. "Wanna meet him?"

"Sure. Why not?" There was no time like the present to get herself back into the swing of things. And the biggest part of her job was making sure every volunteer knew exactly what they were doing. And loved cats.

She set Sophie on the floor and motioned for Angela to lead the way to the curtain that separated the storeroom floor from the back room.

As they walked the twenty feet, she said, "There is one thing I need to tell you before we meet this guy."

Angela nodded.

"The threat on my life, the palace intrigue, the fake marriage, all the drama, sort of reminded everybody that I'm the heir to our throne." She didn't tell Angela the part about her father seeing her only as a placeholder. No need for that to be public. "So I'll be attending more functions in Grennady than I used to be. I won't be spending as much time in America as I have in the past."

Angela stopped walking. "Really?"

"Yeah. But it's okay. Until I'm actually crowned queen, I'll be learning the ropes, spending time with my dad, going to parliament. I can still visit."

Angela laughed. "Okay."

"But my stays will be more like visits than

me being manager. That means you'll be handling things now. Maybe even coordinating between shelters. I'm not quite sure how I'm going to handle it all yet."

Angela laughed. "Is there a raise with this promotion?"

Eva smiled. "Yes. I really appreciate you."

They reached the curtain, which Angela whipped to the side so they could enter. Cat beds lined the floors, along with climbing poles. And cats. At least thirty of them sat, stood or slept somewhere.

And in the center was the new guy, sweeping up.

She couldn't tell if he was gorgeous from the back, but he certainly was tall and built...

Her heart thumped. All the blood seemed to drain from her body. *OMG*.

"What are *you* doing here?"

Broom in hand, Alex turned. "I'm sweeping up."

She wanted to kill him and hug him simultaneously. In his jeans and long-sleeve T-shirt he looked more like a biker than a prince. But he was a prince. A playboy. Somebody who did his duty then disappeared.

"Don't you have a blackjack game somewhere?"

He leaned the broom against the wall. "It's not as much fun as it used to be. You ruined it."

She gaped at him as he walked closer. "*I* ruined it?"

"Yes. I used to be able to play for hours. Now it seems boring without your silly comments."

She laughed. This was her Alex. Her chest loosened. But that only made seeing him all the more difficult. If he expected her to be his friend, she didn't know what she'd do, how she'd handle it. She was barely getting over him as it was. Seeing him every day? It would kill her. "Seriously. What are you doing here?"

"Helping you."

She frowned as he took the final two steps that put him directly in front of her.

"I was also waiting for you to be done with your official business so we could have a proper romance."

Angie leaned toward Eva and whispered, "You know this guy?"

"He's the prince I fake married."

Angie's eyes widened.

"Well, not really," Alex said. "The marriage was very real. Millions watched it on TV."

Wide-eyed, Angie nodded. "I got up at four so I could see it." Her gaze drifted to Alex.

"But you look really different without the red jacket and all those medals."

Alex paid no attention to Angie. "We can't divorce. You'll lose your crown. And you haven't filed for an annulment."

Eva stared at him. "I thought you were filing."

"I'm not the one who needs an annulment."

Her heart thumped again. What did that mean? "So we're still married?"

"Exactly."

Alex faced Angie. "Would you give us a minute?"

Shaking with awe, Angela said, "Sure." But she backed out of the room as if she didn't want to take her eyes off Alex.

And who could blame her. He was every inch a rebel prince.

But that was the problem, wasn't it?

She stepped back, away from him. "Did you come here to tell me you wanted me to file for the annulment?"

"I told you. I'm here to help you."

She sniffed and looked away. He'd hurt her once because she hadn't guarded her heart. She wouldn't be so foolish again.

"Well, sweep up cat fur to your heart's delight. We certainly need the assistance."

She turned away, but he caught her wrist, spun her around and planted his lips on hers.

The kiss was warm and sweet with just a hint of desperation and for a second her heart opened up to the possibility that he didn't just love her, too, he was willing to admit it.

She pulled back, studied his dark wonderful eyes. Her heart actually hurt when she whispered, "What are you doing?"

"Showing you that I'm willing to do whatever needs to be done for you."

"Because?"

"Because I love you."

Her heart stuttered. "And?"

He frowned. "And? You didn't used to be this slow. I don't want the annulment. I want you."

Her heart about melted at that, but there was so much more to this than just not getting a divorce. "My life is constantly in danger, remember? You've lost enough people. You weren't going to be so foolish as to fall in love again."

"About that. Rose reminded me that I've said one or two really stupid things in our time together." He slid his arms around her waist, tugged her to him and kissed her again. One of those soul-melting kisses that weakened her knees and made her want to curl against him and purr.

But she couldn't. She wouldn't. She had to get what she needed from him.

She straightened. "I don't want your fun and games. I want to know this is real. I want somebody to love me."

"I want days like the one we spent at the country house. I want to do things like make pancakes, and just be normal. Add a few kids in there and I think it could be downright wonderful."

She held his gaze. "So do I."

"You know, we could raise an entire family before your dad decides to retire."

She laughed. "Yes. We could."

"We will raise your country's next king, but you'll spend years grooming him because you'll be the best ruler your country has ever seen."

Her heart speeded up, expanded in her chest, blossomed with life it had never had before. "God knows I'll try."

He held out his hand to her. "Do you have an apartment in the city?"

"I do."

"Too bad because my dad booked me an entire floor in a lavish hotel on Fifth Avenue.

Right by the theatre district. Or if you feel like flying, my family owns a casino in Vegas."

She couldn't quite take the hand he offered. She wanted to believe it was real. Did believe in some ways. But it all felt too wonderful. Too perfect. So she laughed. "We can play black-jack."

"We could, but there are other more important things I think we need to do first. Like the one thing we know makes this marriage real. Permanent."

He wanted to make love. Her body shimmied with need. Her heart wanted to burst with anticipation.

But this was huge. Her destiny if he decided it was a mistake or couldn't handle the craziness of her life.

He smiled. "Take my hand. We'll make it. I swear."

She glanced at his hand and back to his face. He was serious.

Everything inside her stilled. She'd been waiting for her prince since she was four, and now here he was, promising what she really wanted. Love. Real love. Total love.

She placed her hand in his. He closed his fingers around it and squeezed. "We're going to have such fun."

"I know."

She felt a shift. A knowing. The years of being a sheltered princess ended and in their place came a real life, a life where she had someone with whom she could be totally honest and somebody who could be honest with her.

He led her to a coatrack where he grabbed a black wool coat and hat. After he slipped into the coat, he kissed her again. "I say we go back to my floor of the hotel, make this a real marriage and then spend our real honeymoon in Vegas."

She nodded.

"After that, it's six months of the year in the country house in Xaviera and six months in your cold but snuggly country."

"What about the cats?"

"We'll keep Angela on staff. Put her in charge of everything."

She tilted her head in amazement. "I sort of already did."

"Then we're set to visit a few times a year. Maybe do a fund-raiser."

As they walked from the back room to the shop floor, she laughed and waved goodbye to Angela, who stared after them as Alex led her out into the world, out into the real life that could be anything they wanted.

Because he had a crown and she had a crown, but right now they had each other and that was all they needed.

* * * * *

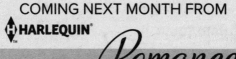

"Dylan, I…"

"What?"

She swung back to him. "I don't know how we can pull
off something like that—pretending to date—convincingly."

She sat again, feeling like a goose for striding around
and revealing her agitation. When she glanced across at him
the expression in his eyes made her stomach flip-flop. In
one smooth motion he slid across until they were almost
touching. He smelled fresh and clean, like sun-warmed
cotton sheets, and her every sense went on high alert.

He touched the backs of his fingers to her cheek and
she sucked in a breath, shocked at her need to lean into the
contact. Oh, this was madness!

"Dylan, I—"

His thumb pressed against her mouth, halting her words.
Then he traced the line of her bottom lip and a pulse thumped
to life inside her. She couldn't stop her lip from softening
beneath his touch, or her mouth from parting ever so slightly
so she could draw the scent of him into her lungs.

"I don't think you realize how lovely you are."

Somewhere nearby a peacock honked. Something splashed in the lily pond. But all Mia could focus on was the man in front of her, staring down at her as if…as if she were a cream bun he'd like to devour…slowly and deliciously.

It shocked her to realize that in that moment she wanted nothing more than to be a cream bun.

Dangerous.

The word whispered through her. Some part of her mind registered it, but she was utterly incapable of moving away and breaking the spell Dylan had weaved around them.

"Sweet and lovely Mia."

The low, warm promise in his voice made her breath catch.

"I think we're going to have exactly the opposite problem. I think if we're not careful we could be in danger of being too convincing… We could be in danger of convincing ourselves that a lie should become the truth."

A fire fanned through her. Yesterday, when he'd flirted with her, hadn't it just been out of habit? Had he meant it? He found her attractive?

"Dylan…" His name whispered from her. She didn't mean it to.

His eyes darkened at whatever he saw in her face. "I dreamed of you last night."

Dangerous.

The word whispered through her again.

But it didn't feel dangerous. It felt right to be whispering secrets to each other.

Don't miss
UNLIKELY BRIDE FOR A BILLIONAIRE,
available August 2016 wherever
Harlequin® Romance books and ebooks are sold.

www.Harlequin.com

Reading Has Its Rewards

Earn **FREE BOOKS!**

Register at **Harlequin My Rewards** and submit your Harlequin purchases from wherever you shop to earn points for free books and other exclusive rewards.

Plus submit your purchases from now till May 30th for a chance to win a $500 Visa Card*.

Visit **HarlequinMyRewards.com** today

Earn **FREE** REWARDS HarlequinMyRewards.com Join Today!

3 1270 00789 2237

MYR16R1